I AM A MAN

DAVID DRAPER

Published in 2016 by FeedARead.com Publishing

Copyright © The author as named on the book cover.

The author or authors assert their moral right under the Copyright, Designs and Patents Act, 1988, to be identified as the author or authors of this work.

All Rights reserved. No part of this publication may be reproduced, copied, stored in a retrieval system, or transmitted, in any form or by any means, without the prior written consent of the copyright holder, nor be otherwise circulated in any form of binding or cover other than that in which it is published and without a similar condition being imposed on the subsequent purchaser.

A CIP catalogue record for this title is available from the British Library.

HOME is where the pain is...Gill Scott-Heron

History is not simply a set of facts or dates but a means by which to comprehend and access the forces of the past that have shaped who we are and the world in which we live......Michael Honey.

PROLOGUE

The phone rang at eight that night. I was watching a British tribute artist well into his fifties mimicking an American pop star on YouTube. The answer machine kicked in.

"Hello Mr Draper. This is Nurse Ratchett ringing from the City Hospital on behalf of George Proctor. George died this afternoon. I was going through his belongings and I came across a brown envelope with your name and telephone number on it. Will you come and pick it up please as soon as possible. You need to make your way to the Fuller1 ward. Thank you."

I didn't know a George Proctor. So I rang the hospital back and spoke to Nurse Ratchett. She told me that my name was the only name they had. He had no relatives that they knew about. I hesitated for a few seconds before agreeing to come. I told her I would pick it up the next day.

The tribute artist was still singing. I turned him off. I didn't sleep well that night. I had disturbing dreams.

Over breakfast the next morning I tried to talk myself out of it. I didn't know a George Proctor. The name meant nothing to me. I had too much to do here and it was pissing down with rain. However, I reasoned with myself, it might be an opportunity missed if I didn't go and the nurse said he had no one else. I know the feeling. The hospital was not too far away from where I lived, but it held bad memories – the last time I had been there was to watch my father die. We didn't get on.

Fuller1 wasn't difficult to find. Nurse Ratchett smiled and handed me the envelope and thanked me for coming. I asked her how George had died.

"He had cancer," she said. I said sorry.

"Don't be," she said, "it wasn't your fault."

I smiled at her, turned and left. It was still raining hard.

I sat in the car outside the hospital and opened the envelope. Inside were a key and a handwritten note. The handwriting was like that of a small child: shaky and barely readable.

> Hello Mr Draper sorry about the writing but that is how it is when you are close to death I got to know about you sometime back through various people on the circuit Norm in particular you interviewed him as part of your research I want to be part of your research the key is the

> house key to my house number 27 Sydenham street Radford you can't miss it it is the one with a green door it has above the door welcome to Graceland go in and walk straight through and into another room there is a table and two chairs on the table is a bigger brown envelope inside the envelope is me for the whole world to see good and

evil black and white and baring my soul
course you could ignore all of it and just go
home but I know you won't because
Priscilla said you wouldn't she said it would
open doors for you like it did for me and you
would find the experience beneficial thank
you for your time.

Priscilla, well, now that was two people in the mix
and she was presuming a lot for somebody who didn't
know me. Norm could be Norman Hall aka Johnny Cash
who I had heard had been found dead a year or two
back. He died in suspicious circumstances apparently. I
didn't know how true that was, though. No one had been
arrested. I had interviewed him as part of my research
for a book I was writing about tribute artists. I was
trying to find out why these people spent their lives
hiding behind the façade of someone else. Norman said
he simply did it for the money and the women. The
women loved it, he said. But for George well it was
something different.

I found 27 Sydenham Street. It had a green door

like George said and it did have "Welcome to Graceland" written above it. It was still raining heavily. Luckily I was able to park outside the house. I made a dash for the door and opened it.

Inside the house there was a distinct smell of paint and detergent. Against the freshly painted bare white wall of the room I entered was a hospital bed stripped of its sheets. I walked on and into the next room. That one too was freshly painted white. I went over to the window that looked out onto a backyard with a wooden fence at the end of it and tried to open it. It wouldn't budge. On the mantelpiece above the fireplace that looked to be a throwback from the seventies – all brick and no character – were three framed photographs. One was of a young woman smiling and wearing a flowered purple dress, another was of a young, good-looking man looking proud and dressed in a grey Italian-designed mohair suit. They both looked to be in their twenties. The third photograph was of two young boys of about twelve standing together with their arms around each other and smiling like they hadn't a care in the world.

Just as George said, in the middle of the room

was a table and chairs, one at each end of the table and on the table was the brown envelope. I picked it up and opened it. I slid out the contents onto the table. There was a manuscript and two photographs. One was of a young Elvis Presley and a black guy. The other was of three black guys standing together looking at the camera. Should I stay and read it there or take it home? I looked at my watch. For reasons I could not explain I decided to stay. I was glad I was wearing my heavy coat because it seemed as if it had got colder.

The title page on the manuscript read I AM A MAN…

I am dying. That is a fact to beat all facts. My consultant told me on the hottest day of the year last year. I said to him, Is that it? He smiled. When will the big day come? You ask. I don't know. Am I bothered, you ask, truly? Well, we'll see. Now, I am on a plane from New York to Memphis; the place I really want be. I will sing in Memphis because my name is Elvis Presley. So what more could I want? My life back? Well, again, we'll see.

I am locked in a dream on this plane from New York to Memphis and in the dream I am sitting on a wonky white toilet seat on a dark, unknown cobbled street that is littered with screeching, indiscreet women and I am in a state of dread trying to have a shite and fearing that they all might stop what they are doing and stare and laugh at my heart beating ten to the dozen and at my hand being swallowed up by my blood and at the crimson bowl beneath me collapsing and at my mam in her new flowered purple dress walking towards me with her beautiful dark hair enveloping her young face and whispering, We will be landing shortly.

Are you okay sir? The fat man sitting next to me asks. I'm okay, thank you for asking. It's been a long day. You were doing some talking fellow. Sorry about that. I didn't know whether to wake you. Sorry. No problem you are from England, right? Yes. Where in England, if you don't mind me asking? I don't mind, a place I called *Home*. He fidgets in his chair and a whiff of his sweat climbs up my nose.

Opposite me, one row down, an older couple wearing red and white baseball caps struggle to give each other a peck on the cheek with their well-worn lips puckered. The peaks of their caps get in the way.

Anywhere near London? I turn to him and his rotund brown face is smiling at me. I stare at the dark mole in the middle of his forehead and say to him, have you had that checked out? He touches his mole and gives off a giggle that does not reflect his size.

I need to wipe the trickles of sweat that are dripping into my eyes. I struggle to take a handkerchief from my trouser pocket, squirming in my seat as I do so. The fat man squirms with me. I'm from Germantown myself. I wipe my eyes. And that's in Memphis? Sure is fellow. Sure is.

The plane hits the ground with a thump and a few bumps then comes to a shuddering stop. Thank god for that, I say under my breath. Amen to that, he says out loud. First time is it? I nod my head. He is not looking. You know I fly to New York at least twice a week. Have been doing so for near on five years yet I still can't get used to it. No sir, every time I step onto a plane my stomach does a 360-degree turn. And like your good self I thank God for getting me home safely.

The old couple, minus baseball hats, give each other a kiss of reassurance. I don't believe in God. The words came out like they do when your body is coming out of a fear zone.

The plane stops. I have arrived. A female cabin crew member in blue, struggles to open the door. There is a lot of shuffling and chattering going on around the cabin as I release myself from the seat and stand up and rescue my hand luggage from the overhead compartment. There is not much in the bag just toiletries, a book about Memphis and my mam's ashes. My head hurts and my back aches badly. A youth squeezes past pushing me back into the seat I had just stood up from. He pats me on the back with an apology and I straighten up again. I am a stranger in town so I don't make a fuss.

Could you oblige me sir and please pass me down the green holdall that has Memphis Redbirds written on it?

The weight of his bag takes me by surprise and, like a magnetic force; it finds its own way down to the seat I had been sitting on. I look at the fat man and cringe an apology. With a slow heavy nod of his head and a wide grin on his face that shows a gap in his mouth where at least two teeth had once sat, he says thanks.

He makes me feel uncomfortable with his smarminess. Did the thanks refer to the passing of the bag or to the expression on my face? It's hard to tell.

Best baseball team in the whole of the United States. I bet you follow soccer. I don't answer him. I just give a slight grin, while in my head I am telling him to go away and leave me alone. I just want to get off the plane, get to the hotel and get my head down.

I remember the jolly woman in the Co-op travel shop on Angel Row telling me to try and stay up until at least midnight their time. That way, she said, your sleep pattern isn't broken and jet lag won't kick in. You will be able to enjoy the rest of your holiday without feeling tired all the time, she said. I said, It's easier said than done when you're dying, and I smiled and she smiled back but not in the same way.

Along with rest of the passengers I shuffle my way to the front of the plane. I had been sitting near the back. I am in front of the fat man and he is speaking to the back of my head. David and Victoria, now there are a couple of guys I respect. His hot breath is so close to my left ear it begins to warm up. I got a glimpse of them one day on Fifth Street, shopping, course David had about three or four bags dangling from his arms.

Was it three or was it four and does it really matter? I say to myself. He continues, I recognised them from the newspaper. They seem a nice couple. What does he mean they seem a nice couple? I ask him, did you speak to them? No I didn't, he said. It seems a strange thing to say, I think. They seemed a nice couple. Have you, sir? What, I replied. Spoken to them, he said. I can only respond with a tired, No, wishing the man would stop yapping. He is setting my head on fire.

We are only a third of the way down the aisle and already I can feel the heat of the day coming in through the open door. Perspiration is leaking out of my hair. You have picked a hot one fellow and that's for sure. This time of year the temperature, round these parts especially, can go through the roof, yes sirree. A male voice, further back, responds with an Amen to that.

At the exit door, a dark-haired, well-proportioned young woman is smiling and wishing us all well and reminding us to mind the steps as we leave the plane. The fat man behind me says, you too, Miss. A voice behind him says, Amen to that. I stumble slightly

Once inside the mobile tunnel I look at my watch and realise I have not altered the time. It's been twelve hours on the move from Gatwick to Memphis. Considering that back home I would now be in bed, I feel surprisingly lively. The woman in the travel shop had done her homework. I bet the naps I have been taking on the way here have helped except the last one that was deep and scary too. Any more where that came from I wonder, we'll have to wait and see.

I present my passport to the well-dressed young man standing at the door. He looks at it then looks at me. He looks at it again then looks at me again. He looks at it again, looks at me again then hands it back to me with a smile. I understand. Some people laugh out loud but that's their problem not mine.

The interior of the airport is clean and brown, with small brick pillars and a low ceiling. The arrival and departure gates and waiting areas run down the left side of the building. After a short walk, passed all the activity of comings and goings, the airport widens out and presents you with a shopping mall. I stop. Now confusion sets in. To the left and to the right of the shop in front of me, I forget what it was – sweet shop, clothes shop, newsagent – are two walkways with people rushing up and down them both. Which way do I go to the carousel? There is no sign. I need a sign. It's hot, I am sweating like a stuffed pig and the new blue denim jacket is sticking to my back. Perhaps it was me I could smell on the plane. Perhaps it wasn't the fat man at all. You know what they say about pigs. Follow me, the voice behind me says.

It makes me jump. I bet I know why you're in Memphis. Sorry sir I didn't mean to surprise you, it says. I turn round and the grinning, rotund face of the man from the plane is staring at me. You didn't, I reply without smiling back. In fact, I am glad to see him and I walk on beside him and he is surprisingly nimble for a man of his size. I hadn't noticed before how tall he is, I am looking up at him.

You know without this fortnight you people spend here in August celebrating his death, Memphis would be near broke. Yes sir the money that is generated by you folk is manna from heaven for us poor folk here in Shelby County. Shelby County? I say quizzically. Yes sir, Memphis is in Shelby County. Memphis Tennessee is a great place to be. The man gives off a raucous laugh. Hey not bad if I do say so myself. Are you singing?

Us folk sounds wrong. I can see the carousel in the distance ahead of me. I hurry on towards it, leaving the man behind. Us folk, it sounds kind of derogatory. I know what he means, but it sounds wrong all the same. Still, he could have said you fans. Now that would have made me want to smack him one. I'm more than a fan.

Okay, you have a great time now, do you hear. I turn around and the man is holding his hand out for me to shake. Considering how big he is he looks remarkably cool in his blue checked sports coat. I, on the other hand, like I have already said, am sweating like a stuffed pig, so I am embarrassed to shake the hand he holds out. I wipe mine down my trouser leg in a frenzied attempt to dry it. Can I ask you sir are you performing? He asks again. I don't want to answer him why well that's my choice ain't it. The area is near deserted but for a few elderly ladies standing up close having a chin wag and not taking much notice of the sparse number of bags that are making their way round the carousel. I cannot yet see mine.

Are you taking part? Why does he want to know? Should I say yes or should I say no. I watch the bags slowly move on their way. The old ladies have moved closer to the carousel. My bag is not there. I panic. It's been left in New York; you here about these things. A fellow in a pub told me once about how it happened to him one year in Benidorm. His suitcase was missing the whole week he was there. He had to buy some new clothes. It was waiting for him when he landed back at the airport. He said he sued but lost his case. I laughed. He didn't see the funny in what he said so he threw a punch instead and called me a cripple. He missed. I didn't.

So you have a good time then, hey? Yes, I reply, the word coming out fast and harsh. I turn and try to apologise. It's my bag; I can't go on without it. The man smiles and grips my arm in a consoling way, don't you worry now, it'll be along soon. The old black boys back there they don't rush none. He whispers up close, it's in their blood. You know what I mean? He turns and walks away quickly, like a naughty boy who has just snitched on somebody at infant school and doesn't want to get caught. He heads for the exit sign.

It's six thirty. Half past twelve at home. I take off my blue denim jacket and drop it to the floor. I hold tight onto my well-worn brown bag by swinging it across my shoulders, don't want to leave my mam's ashes behind. You don't know what might happen. She might start singing. I reach into the pocket of my brand new pair of blue Wranglers that I bought especially for the trip and retrieve the already damp handkerchief from the pocket and mop my face with it.

The chatty old ladies disperse with their luggage, leaving me standing alone; alone. The carousel stops. There is a song there somewhere. Alone, why must I be alone? Alone, yes you'd think I would be used to it by now. Who sang it? A one hit wonder else I'd remember.

I look around me and the area is deserted but for me and an old black guy in green overalls, sweeping the floor like he is in a slow dance with a beautiful lady. His head is down and it looks like he is in no hurry to finish; like he has no place to go. He comes up closer, his brush head now about a foot away from where I'm standing. I don't move and he doesn't look up. Behind him, on a well-polished cream wall, are two photographs side by side. One is of the King and the other is of Martin Luther. What is he doing there? They are both smiling and looking directly at me. But I can't be sure.

The man with the brush stops what he is doing, stretches up and smiles at me, leaning lazily on the handle. You gonna move mister? He asks. I tell him, I'm waiting for my bag. He laughs. His laugh is so loud it echoes. A lot of noise from a man as old as he is, I think. What, he must be eighty at least. Man, he says, I have been waiting for my bag since the day I was born.

His presence, his demeanour, makes me feel vulnerable. I'm thinking, I'm easy pickings for anyone who wants to jump me. I move closer to the carousel and apologise to the old man. He's still laughing. He carries on sweeping and this is Memphis: Mecca, the home of rock 'n' roll.

The airport feels like it's getting smaller. I sit down on the edge of the carousel to steady myself. It feels like I am in that dream, naked and exposed. I wish the big man had waited with me. He would have helped. A clattering noise disturbs the silence and the carousel starts up again. And there it is, my bag, wrestling with the leather flaps it has to pass through before it reaches its destination. My shoulders drop with relief and I smile a little as I pick up my jacket from the floor and go and rescue my bag from the moving belt.

I turn and walk in the same direction the fat man did. The man with the brush shouts after me, Mister, Memphis ain't just about white men singing the blues. I look at my watch it's just past six thirty. I keep on walking and half turn and shout back, Thank you. No sir, he shouts, you'll soon see that it ain't. I sense a slight spring in my step.

I go through the automatic doors and enter what looks like a massive bus station. Only there are no buses just yellow taxis scattered randomly. I walk on and come to a taxi rank with a few people waiting. I stand behind them and wait my turn. I do not notice the fat man standing a few people down. Hello again. I drop my bag to the floor while I wait and look in the direction of the voice.

Sounding like a quiz show host he shouts, Come on down fellow and stand with me. I feel embarrassed at his request and look at the faces of the people standing in front of me. Come on, these good people don't mind. I look at them for confirmation and in unison they all smile and nod their heads. Embarrassed, I pick up my bag and walk to the man.

I feel relieved and safe with the knowledge that he is here. I relax a little. There is a cheeky grin on his face as he leans in close to me. (He does smell.) He says, didn't I tell you? I don't ask him what he means. He stands up straight again and in a more direct tone, that sounds like a statement of intent, he tells me I am going to share the taxi with him. Instinctively I reply that it doesn't matter, although, deep down, I'm thankful for the offer. All I want to do is get to the hotel and the big man, I'm sure, is going to make this happen.

Nonsense man, I know where I'm going and you don't. I'm assuming it's your first trip to Memphis. Yes it is, I reply more feebly than I would have liked. So, mister, we want to make you feel welcome. Don't we folks? He turns to the people standing behind me and, like a preacher rousing his congregation, he raises his arms in the air and, together, they all cry out, Amen to that.

Besides, didn't you say you were staying at the Crown? I reply, I don't think so. I may have done. I can't remember. Okay, anyways it's on my way home so it's no trouble. Thank you, I appreciate it. Oh don't mention it brother. We Memphis folk, well some of us anyways, if you get my drift, are here to take care of them that needs it.

A yellow taxi pulls up alongside us. A black man leaves the driving seat and walks to the back of the car. Me and the big man are already there. The black man is wearing a green tweed suit. He opens up the boot, picks up my bag first and puts it in. With a bit more effort he picks up the fat man's bag and groans, Jesus man, what you got in this thing, your girlfriend? The fat man's laugh sounds genuine as he gets into the back seat. Because I don't know what the hell they are talking about, as I squeeze in next to the big man, my giggle is less genuine.

The highway leads to the shadowy tip of reality...you are on a through route to the land of the different, the bizarre, and the unexplainable. Go as far as you like on this road. Its limits are only those of mind itself.......Rod Serling.

Where to folks? The Crown, please Henry. He says it like the driver was his own personal chauffeur. Henry in turn says *Nice*, in a not quite falsetto voice that befits the age he looks. It is sort of squeezed out. He tells me later that he is seventy-four. The same age the King would have been if he had lived. The taxi pulls away.

My stomach feels queasy. I can't tell if it's because I haven't eaten properly since leaving England, or because I am in the only place I've ever wanted to be since I was twelve years of age or is it because I feel scared. Not of death, no, I don't have any issues about death; or where I'm going when it comes – heaven or hell – because I don't believe in either; or when it will happen; or where I'll be when it does happen. The doctors can't give me a straight answer no, not here, not now, no. So we will just have to wait and see.

We are driving down Dr Martin Luther King Avenue – strange word to use, Avenue, for a Highway that looks to be twice the size of our own motorways. Henry is whistling a tune that belongs to the King; Love Me, which is weird because that's my favourite. That is the one I intend to sing later.

Let me fill you in. It was on January 31, 1968 when everything changed. You could say it was a happening. I was twelve years old and already a criminal, we robbed gas meters me and my best friend Norm. Anyways, I had just got in from the pictures in town with Norm. A film called *If*. It was an eighteen certificate but Norm had an uncle who worked at the Gaumont and he let us in for nothing, through the side door.

I had a strop on when I got home because I wanted to be at Norm's place. His mam and dad were having a party. But I promised my mam I would stay in with her. My dad was out at the Variety Club on Salisbury Street. It was his local. My mam didn't go in for that sort of thing anymore. She was a devout stay-at-home woman. She took care of the home. She used to go out when they were younger, usually on a Saturday night, but she just stopped. She told me later, near the end, why. It came as no surprise. Always thought something was going on.

I can see her now, plonked on the sofa, squeezed up in the corner, her favourite spot, and wearing her flowered purple dress staring at the television. The special had just started. Come and sit here beside me, she said, patting the cushion next to her. What you watching? I asked her. My mam looked at me and smiled. I liked her smile. She was a very attractive lady was my mam. God knows why my dad did what he did. She said, the one and only of course. Up to that moment the one and only to me was only heard when she put his records on and then she would only listen to him when my dad was not in. He hated him with a vengeance said he was a big girl's blouse and had a voice like an alley cat. Jealousy can do things to people.

The fat man asks me if I am in Memphis for the duration. Duration, what sort of word is that, I think. It sounds like I'm going to war or something. I turn to him and apologise. I don't know why. Where are we? I ask. Henry says, Highway 50. Dr Martin Luther King Avenue. The greatest— but the fat man jumps in, cutting Henry short. Over that way to my right is Little

Rock and over there to your left is Arkansas and up ahead to the right is Nashville.

In the driving mirror Henry's dark eyes are staring at me.

And over there to your left is Highway 51. That one will take you all the way to Graceland. I already know that. Does the fat man think I wouldn't know that?

Three seven one seven; Highway 51 to be precise, Henry says in a confident tone of voice. The fat man contradicts him in a schoolmasterly way. No sir you are wrong; it is three seven six four. Henry is staring at me, this time with a twinkle in his eyes. No sir, it is you that is wrong, he says. I should know, man, I have spent enough time there. We all sit in a heavy depressing silence for a few seconds.

Then I say, It's a big place so could you both be right? You been there, brother? Henry asks. I reply, with a shaky, No, I haven't. So, what you said doesn't make sense. Ain't that right or ain't it?

He takes me by surprise by asking my name. Why? I think. Why does he want to know my name? My name is George Montgomery, the fat man says. We knows that George. I'm asking the man here what his name is. I don't think that, Henry has anything to do with you. Oh, and why not George? He knows mine, he knows yours, I know yours and youse know mine so.

They sound like two school kids bickering over I don't know what. At first I don't want to say. But then I think, Sod it I'm dying so I say, with confidence, my name, Henry, George, is Elvis Presley. The expected silence happens. George breaks the silence. Elvis, well what about that, he says.

I sit staring out of the window at the passing cars. I should make myself aware of where I am, but instead what has just been said between us is creeping me out. The silence is not unusual. It happens when I'm in the company of people not on the circuit. George again breaks the silence. Well, your parents, he goes on, must have liked him a lot to do that.

I stare out the window whilst I speak to them. I catch my reflection through the glass. My dad hated him. My mother thought he was the best thing on two legs. I see the signs for Little Rock and Nashville. Henry joins in the conversation. Man that must have been awkward. Not really it was my choice.

Henry asks, Can you sing? I begin to fidget a little. I don't want to answer that one but I do. I get by,

I say. We are staring at each other through his driving mirror. There is intensity in his eyes which is challenging. I give in and look away. Henry carries on talking. What I reckon is this, if youse are called Elvis Presley, like you said you were… I am, that is my name, I tell him again. Then all I'm saying is that you'd better have a voice to match man. Otherwise you are doing the fellow no favours.

Something is stirring inside me. My adrenaline is on the move. I return my gaze to his mirror but he isn't there. I want to say something nasty but I don't know what and I'm scared. George settles things down. He says to Henry, I don't think you're being fair there Henry. I'm just giving off my point of view George that's all. It's a free country now, ain't it? I can do that now can't I, me being black anall. It was the last time I looked, George says. Don't mean any harm by it Elvis. None taken Henry, I say.

I've got butterflies in my stomach. I'm hoping that we can get to the hotel without another word being spoken, but I'm sure that's not going to happen with these two in the car. It sounds to me like these two have history. I have visions of an O.K. Corral scenario – a black on white or a white on black shooting with me as the only witness and alone in a place that, in my dreams, is paradise but could become hell on earth very quickly.

I've got my nose pinned up against the car door window. The heat from outside feels like it's swallowing me up. Henry is quietly whistling but loud enough for me to hear clearly my favourite song. Out the corner of my eye I can see George staring at me. Without turning round to face him I ask him, when does it get cooler? It doesn't get cool man it just gets dark, Henry says, laughing. George adds, you never get accustomed neither, not outsiders anyway, Henry says, they just fry. And they both laugh. The tone of conversation suggests that things have settled back down. I try to do the same.

The taxi stops at green boxed traffic lights that are hanging in the air swinging on a pole. A group of young black men descend on the taxi. Henry winds down his window and gets into conversation with them. The light changes to green. The driver in the car behind us sits with his hand stuck to the horn of his car. George is noticeably fidgety and I just wish I wasn't here. He leans forward and taps Henry on his shoulder. He says, hey fella, they've changed and then sits back. After a minute or two of banter between Henry and the other guys, they disperse, letting out a scream of laughter that would wake the dead.

Henry pulls away, chuckling to himself. The car behind draws level and screams expletives at us through the open window of his car. Henry is oblivious to him and George shrugs his shoulders and points a finger at the back of Henry's head. George leans up close to me and whispers, didn't I tell you Elvis? They wanna bomb up their butts, you know what I mean.

Henry is still giggling as we drive into a more populated area. George tells me that we are on Main Street South. This, my man, is where they all start swarming like bees, Henry says. And it looks like he is right. The area is heaving with Elvi's just meandering to the left and to the right of the taxi and walking in the middle of the road, oblivious to what traffic there is around them. Henry does some meandering of his own scattering the pests as he slowly moves down Main and past the famous Orpheum Theatre, one of the many places in Memphis where the King shone his light.

Pulling into the hotel car park, Henry is whistling a slow melodic tune. He stops close to the main entrance. Still whistling the same tune, he gets out of the car and walks to the back. Later I ask him what the tune is and he tells me it belongs to Mae. A strange title I think.

Before getting out I ask George how much I owe him. He tells me not to worry. He's smiling as he says it. I insist on paying. He chuckles and says that this one is on him. You can pay next time, he says. I say under my breath, what next time? He reaches into his coat pocket, takes out a small card and hands it to me. How long did you say you were staying for? I didn't. Well I don't think I did. I take his card and leave the taxi, turn and thank him again. Give me a call. I'll show you around. He smiles.

I close the door and walk to the back of the car where Henry is standing, still whistling the same tune and waiting to hand me my bag. I say to him, that's a nice tune, he smiles. He's not as tall as he looks seated behind his wheel, slightly shorter than me, in fact. His face is well worn and he is now wearing a baseball hat that has *I Am A Man* written on it. He hands me the bag. I take it but he doesn't release it. He looks at me and pulls me and the bag closer to him I grip it tighter. He whispers, He was my friend. I can smell garlic on his breath. He whispers the words again then releases the handle of the bag leaving me shaken but not stirred. Who? I ask, surprised at his outburst. He just smiles and says calmly, you know, you know.

Rather clumsily I tell him that George will pay him the fare and I hand him a dollar. He refuses it. The woman in the travel agency back home told me that tipping in this part of the world is normal. Henry waves it away and walks back to his car. I want to ask him if I have offended him in some way. Keep it, fellow, you never know when you might need it. My name is Henry Fuller. We will meet again. I watch the taxi pull away with his name ringing in my ear.

At the door of the hotel, a tall black man wearing a green uniform and an oversized green peaked hat on his head meets me and indicates to me with a hand movement that he wants to take my bag. I tell him that it doesn't matter because it isn't heavy and thank him for asking. The expression on his face quickly changes from a smile to a frown and he blocks my way by holding his hand out, expressing more forcefully his wish to take my bag. He tells me that it is his job to carry my bag. I hand it to him. He thanks me and I follow him into the hotel and up to the reception desk.

At the desk he carefully places my bag onto the floor between us both and waits with me whilst the receptionist takes my details. Good evening sir and welcome to the Crown. The man carrying your bag tonight is Benny he's one of our many bellboys who are here to assist you in any way they can. I think, strange word, bellboy. Benny must be well into his sixties if not older. I turn to Benny, smile, nod and whisper an apology. I don't know why. It seems I am doing a lot of apologising today. Benny does likewise – nods his head I mean.

Now let us get you booked in so you can begin to enjoy your stay here in Memphis. Can you give me your name please sir. It's Elvis Presley. As I expect, the man, behind the desk, with his obviously dyed jet black hair, stops what he is doing and looks at me curiously. Can I see your passport please sir? I open it at the relevant place and hand it to him. There you are, I say, Elvis Presley. I was born on the 22nd January, 1957. I'm Aquarius too. No words are spoken between us whilst the well-groomed receptionist, whose name I can see on his name tag is Hank, checks his computer screen before filling in the rest of the form.

The pain in my back has got worse. The doctor said it would. The longer I go without taking the tablets the worse the pain will get, that is what he said. I haven't taken any since New York and I don't intend to take any whilst I'm here.

I turn to Benny, who is looking the other way, and ask him if has worked at the hotel for long. For a long time sir, he says. He turns to face me and smiles. Several gold teeth sparkle like stars.

Expressionless, Hank says, Thank you Elvis and passes back my passport. As I majestically slip the passport back into the pocket of my well-worn, blue denim jacket I ask him, with a tone of superiority in my voice, if everything is okay. Hank nods and pushes one of them fancy cards that open your hotel room door towards me. I say to Hank, I got into bother with one of these in a hotel I was staying at in Birmingham. He says, with a surprised look on his face, Birmingham, Alabama? And I say, No, Birmingham, England. I just could not get the connection right between the green light that comes on when you push the card into the slot and the opening of the door. I struggled with it the whole of the weekend I was there. Hank tells me not to worry too much about it. He says, We don't want this little biddy thing, he waves it in front of me, to come between you and your stay here now do we no sir. No, we want you to not think about anything else but the many pleasures Memphis can bring, Elvis. Benny here will show you what to do. Room four nine two please Benny.

As I scoop up the key from the desk, I say with an even bigger smile, under my breath, Go fuck yourself Hank, then bend down to pick up my bag only to be beaten to it by Benny.

Benny turns and heads for the lift and like a little puppy dog I follow him. We step into one of those glass lifts. You know the all-glass ones which enable you to see what is happening below. My stomach doesn't like it. It will be all right if I don't look down.

Number four nine two is on the fourth floor, ten rooms down from the lift. All the rooms along the narrow corridor have typical brown teak doors. The floor is covered in a shocking red-patterned carpet that looks new. The walls are painted marigold with photographs of the King hanging on them. Benny opens the door with his own key and walks in.

He places the bag down on the floor next to the bed, which is close to the window, and waits. I say,

Thank you Benny, and make my way to the large window which overlooks the streets below behind the hotel. It's the first thing I do when I find myself in unfamiliar surroundings. I don't know why. Benny doesn't move. Then I realise why he doesn't move. I haven't tipped him – Henry not taking what I offered him has thrown me. I walk towards him apologising for my oversight whilst trying to rescue some dollar notes from my trouser pocket. I say, Sorry, I'm a bit screwed up, when what I meant to say was, sorry; they are a bit screwed up. I hand him a dollar. Before taking it he smiles, touches the peak of his oversized hat and says, Thank you sir. I thank him in return and follow him to the door. He is giggling and muttering to himself, Birmingham, England. He leaves and I close the door behind him.

My back is hurting and I want to lie down but I daren't. I will fall asleep. I'm alone. It is just me in a hotel room in Downtown Memphis, alone. Alone in a room that looks out over Lauderdale Courts – Lauderdale Courts, where the King lived. I am standing and staring and imagining him as a fair-haired, spotty-faced teenager, walking the brown concreted complex lost, whilst his mam is indoors whittling herself silly on his whereabouts, like my mam whittled herself silly when her own spotty-faced kid was out with Norm robbing gas meters.

I find my shoulder bag and take out my mam's ashes, which are enshrined in a small red casket, and place them next to the window pane. I take out the blue guidebook and read her the passage that tells us that the city fathers at one time were thinking of knocking down the courts. But Lauderdale Courts, apartment 328, 185 Winchester, saved the day. It was where the King settled when he first moved up from Tupelo, Mississippi with his mam and dad. That's got to stand for something. So they reinvented the courts and turned it into a high technology complex with its own secured gate and fence. Now they rent out the King's apartment to anybody who is willing to pay the price. But, if you want to stay there, you have to book it at least two years in advance. Two years ago my head was somewhere else.

The night is drawing in and I'm starting to feel hungry and it still feels very warm. The last time I ate was in New York waiting for the flight to Memphis. It was an hour late so I had a chilli hot dog. I'd forgotten to take a sickness pill. The chilli hot dog lay in my stomach for half an hour. That is about right these days. The doctor said no more spicy stuff. But he also said no Memphis.

Where is this Germantown? I search the blue book for an answer. It's probably where the well-heeled posh American lives if George is anything to go by. Like, I imagine, The Park back home. I find it. It is, like George said, a suburb of Memphis. Like Radford, where I live, is a suburb of Nottingham. It is not far from downtown Memphis where I am now. Down town that's what we used to say when I was growing up. Where you going Norm? Down town are you coming? I put the blue book next to my mam's ashes. It is something for you to read while I'm out, I tell her. Before leaving the room, I check myself in the mirror: Need a little sun on my back, I think.

The reception area is quiet considering the time of year. I scan the place hoping more than ever I don't catch the eye of an Elvi. An Elvi, if you have not gathered by now, is a fan of the King. I am not a fan. Neither am I good in these situations. I want to be on my own. I prefer it that way; I'm not good at small talk.

I make my way to an eating area that is close to the reception desk and enter. It is more a pub than a restaurant with the bar circling the centre of the room and the eating area hugging the walls around it. I sit down at a table with four chairs and look at the large menu that is open in front of me. The choice is overwhelming with every meat burger you could think of. Good evening sir.

I look up and looking down at me is a young woman; she is smiling a gorgeous smile. She wears the traditional white top and black skirt. I say, Evening, and blush. I drop my head and bury it inside the menu. Can I get you a drink whilst you make your mind up? She asks. And like a shy little boy I reply yes okay. What can I get you? Can I have a beer, please? What kind of beer sir? I look up at her and she is still smiling. It's not a fake smile either. You can tell fake smiles. I have seen lots of fake smiles in my time. Lorrie, my wife, was good at it. I say, you tell me. Do you want a large cold beer or a small cold beer? Large or small, that's what I asked my doctor; is it a large tumour or a small tumour? A large cold one, I say. She smiles and walks away.

My watch says eight thirty. It's the middle of the night back home. I would never eat in the middle of the night. I am struggling to make a choice: chips and burger; spare rib burger and chips; chips and pizza covered in peperoni. I hate peperoni. The words on the menu are morphing into one great dollop. I am reminded of the chilli hot dog.

I don't know whether it's because I am starting to feel tired or if it is all the travelling I have done today – well, yesterday to be precise. I had to stay in a hotel overnight at the airport in London, which was actually the day before that. Or perhaps it is the thought of eating, but I feel nauseous, sweaty and dizzy. So I get up to leave.

I nearly knock the young lady over. I grab her arm. It feels warm. I can feel her breath on my face. It smells sweet. I can smell Magnolia. I let go and apologise. We are face to face. Her black, swept-back, hair tied up in a bun catches my eye. Lorrie my ex-wife, would wear her hair in the same way when she was working.

The young girl has a large frothy beer in her hand and she is smiling. She says, your beer sir. I want to ask her to say it again. I half-heartedly smile back at her wondering if her lips are as warm and soft as her arm. I turn back to the table and put two dollar notes down on top of the menu, say sorry again and leave, brushing her arm as I do so. I go outside into the warm air.

There is a fountain outside. I lean against its wall. The humidity is gripping. I rinse my face in the water. The water is cold and soothing. Tomorrow I will be on a stage somewhere in this town singing my favourite song.

Lorrie said to me once that I had a basic fear of women. What did she mean by basic fear? I asked her, and she said I subconsciously fear women. I said to her, I don't fear you, and she said to me, yes you do. If you didn't, she said, you would commit yourself fully to me. Instead, she said, I have to share you with the King. She didn't want to do that and I couldn't stop. I wanted them both. I am greedy that way

I wonder if the young woman knows anybody who knew the King. As if I'm going to ask her. I bet there will be loads of people around this week earning tons of cash from telling their stories. Most of them made up, I bet.

For a main street this one is quiet – just the sound of the water – and I don't feel nauseous anymore. It's nine o'clock, the moon is up, the stars are out and my wet tee-shirt is clinging to me like a straight jacket. I can hear a rumbling sound. It is a yellow trolley bus travelling up Main Street towards me and it stops opposite me. I watch it stop.

The worst aspect of our time is Prejudice…Rod Serling

There is a black face at every window of the yellow trolley bus and they are staring at me. Why are they staring at me with their long faces? It's perhaps not good for me to be standing around in the dark on my own. I watch the clangety-clangety trolley bus pull away. A black guy a green tweed suit is standing at the stop. He crosses the road and, with a stiff back and striding gait, walks towards me grinning from ear to ear. I check my back pocket for my wallet; turn and walk quickly back into the hotel.

Once inside I stop, turn and look. He is at the door waving his hand at me. He shouts, How you doin' Elvis. It's that Henry fellow. Why is he standing at the door? Is he waiting for me to go to him? Does he want me to go to him? Do you want that drink now sir?

I jump with surprise and turn to see the young woman smiling that beautiful smile at me. I'm sorry, I say, you made me jump. She gently takes my arm. Her fingers feel hot against my flesh. She whispers, I'm sorry I did that to you. I splutter, you didn't do anything to me. She releases my arm and says, I'll see you tomorrow. She smiles, winks, turns and walks away.

Hello! Sorry. She stops and turns round to face me. I want to shout her back and ask her to take my arm like she did just then and repeat what she said like she did just then but instead I say, Sorry, about earlier I mean. She says, there are a lot of sorrys going around tonight, and I say, smiling, there are a lot of smiles going round too. Then I say, trying to catch her sympathy, hoping she might come back, it's probably the jet lag and I felt I needed some fresh air. But instead she steps back and says, in a more formal way, that's okay, I understand. Bye now. And she turns and leaves.

I watch her leave the hotel. She has her hair down and is now wearing orange slacks and a luminous green top. I've seen that combination before on my mam when I was a kid. She was sitting in her favourite spot on the sofa sobbing like a baby listening to the King singing Love Me. I asked her what was up and she grabbed my arm and squeezed it till it hurt.

Once outside, she kisses Henry on his cheek and hooks her arm into his and together they walk away. I rush to the door and watch them walk down Main

Street, all cuddled up and cosy like. I watch them till they are out of sight. Who would have thought?

Feeling pathetic and stupid, I go back into the bar and sit at the same table I had sat at before. This time Stanley is my waiter for the night. Stanley is a middle-aged, hair-receding, bent-back white fellow. I ask him for a large cold beer. American football is on the television above the bar. The sound is turned down. No one seems interested in the pictures. I'm not either. I tried to watch it once back home in my own house – the one I grew up in; I moved back in after the divorce – but couldn't get my head round the rules.

Stanley doesn't smile; probably been at it for too long. He's well weather worn and looks to be in his forties. He puts me in mind of Tom Waits. He passes me a large beer and I ask him how much and he tells me I don't pay until I'm ready to leave. I ask him, Stanley, do you like the King? The what? He says in a high pitched voice. The King Stanley, do you like the King? He responds immediately in a deep Southern drawl, No sir I do not. He says it without looking at me, and turns and walks to the next table. There is nothing for it. I decide to get pissed.

I am having a dream I am in the house I grew up in and a young girl is shouting mumbo jumbo at me. I cannot see her I can only hear her and I am trying to dress myself in front of a massive television screen. It is showing *Gunsmoke*, the Western, in black and white; my dad is shouting at me from inside the television to move, Marshall Matt Dillon is pointing a gun at him and I am getting tangled up in my clothes and falling over. Elvis are you ready? I shout back, Hang on, I'm coming. She shouts, Hurry man, else we will be late. And I shout, for what? You know for what Elvis, come on now. Henry is waiting; you know he wants to see you. I shout, but what about Doctor Montgomery? I've got to see Doctor King. Doctor King is dead Elvis, you know that. I fall over and onto my mam who is lying on the settee open-mouthed wearing her new purple flowered dress. She swings her arms round me and I can't move, my breath is being squeezed from me and the young woman is screaming, Be careful Elvis, she will sqeeze you to death.

 I wake up with my body lost in a forest of sheets and my pores oozing a river shouting, I'm sorry, I'm sorry. The sun is melting the room. I was that pissed when I climbed into the sack last night, I forgot to switch the air conditioning on.

From where I lie I can see Lauderdale Courts in bright sunshine. I ease myself up and rest my back against the wall, stretch up my arm and throw a switch that is on the wall behind me. I hear a gentle purring sound and feel cold air raining down on me. It feels weird. I look at my watch. It's ten thirty. Not too bad. Lauderdale will be my first point of call, then the Sun Studios and last, but not least, Graceland. In between I will be singing.

I take a shower. The thermometer on the wall reads thirty degrees. I've never been anywhere this hot before. The doctor said to me, don't drink too much alcohol, and I said to him, Okay, and it was my intention whilst here not to, but the woman was beautiful. He didn't seen her if he had he would sympathise he would say, Okay go ahead.

The warm spray of water is teasing my nerve ends. My body responds and I'm a spent youth again. I say thank you and stay still for a few seconds to let my breathing settle down. I think it is going to be a beautiful day.

I unpack, and hang the few clothes I brought with me in the brown wardrobe, leaving out my jeans and a plain pink tee-shirt. I hate motifs on tee-shirts as much as I hate modern designer names. Norm called it the start of corporate fascism. We would rummage mainly in charity shops but it wasn't easy finding plain stuff. Once dressed, I check myself in the long mirror that hangs on the wardrobe door. It is something I have to do before leaving any room. Where there is a mirror I look into it. It is something I have done since I was a kid in short pants. Norm says I must be insecure. I said to him, I don't think so and we both laughed. I just know it is important to me. I think I need to know I still exist. I say bye to my mam and leave.

I look for the breakfast room, which I was told is on the top floor. I take the stairs. The lift makes me nervous. Through the doors at the top of the stairs is a sign directing me to the breakfast room, which is tiny considering how big the hotel is. There are the usual things on display, cereals, juice, bread, eggs, sunny side up, whatever that means. I notice a table is free against the window. I hate walking into a room by myself and finding out that I have to share a table with someone else. I would rather leave than sit down with a total stranger. You feel you are obliged to say something and probably they are too. I sit down with my orange juice. I'm not hungry.

In the distance is a white pyramid-shaped building, homage to Egypt, I believe. The name Memphis comes from Egypt, so it says in the blue book. It also says that the bridge I can see spanning the wide Mississippi takes you to Arkansas, the birth place of Johnny Cash. It is called the Hernando de Soto Bridge; who Hernando de Soto is, the blue book doesn't say. Johnny Cash must have come across that bridge when he first came to Memphis to try his luck with Sam Phillips. Norm would have loved this. He would have wet himself being where Johnny Cash had been.

Two Japanese kids sit down at a table opposite me. They block my view of the bridge. I catch their eye and they smile that big broad Japanese smile and nod and shout across the table at me, Elvis Presley? I nod back and smile. Poor sods, how little they know. They stand up and show me the tee-shirts they are wearing. They are identical and have on them the broody, handsome face of the King. The kids look to be in their teens and straight out of Jarmusch's *Mystery Train*. I smile and carry on drinking my juice. I can hear their chatter and feel good about the fact that his message is reaching the young; long live the King. The juice is cold and sweet. I will pay, I thought, and I do.

Nothing ever changes. It doesn't matter where I am in the world, I cannot get away with only having one shit in the morning: one before breakfast, one after breakfast. The world, by the way, is an exaggeration. My visits have usually restricted themselves to the east coast of England: Bridlington, Scarborough, Whitby and, of course, Skegness. Most of my childhood was spent in Skegness. At the miners' holiday camp for two weeks of the year: the beach in the day, or the arcades if it was raining, and the social in the evening. The old man, with a few beers inside him, would do a turn. He had a good voice, a Mario Lanza type voice and my mam would sit, gooey-eyed, with her gin and tonic. That was then before it all changed.

Back on my corridor I see the cleaners lurking. It's panic time. Should I stay or should I go? If I leave there is the chance of me getting caught short. It's the nature of the beast they say. If I stay the cleaners might come into my room while I'm dropping the babies off. Then I will panic and shut up shop. I make a dash down the stairs and find another toilet in the reception area.

But I still can't relax. There are a lot of people coming and going. I am struggling to let go. Nothing will flow. I wait and things start to settle down much like false contractions so I believe. Lorrie would have said you don't know a thing about proper pain.

The reception area is busy with the arrival of new Elvi's. Hordes of them are surrounding the desk where Hank stands. Hasn't he been home? Benny is standing at the door. He is holding it open for people to pass through. I ask him the directions to Lauderdale Courts. Go behind that church you see over there. He is not looking in the direction of the church but looking scornfully at a young white kid who has just stepped on his foot and not apologised. Do you mean that church Benny? I point at the one I could see from my bedroom window. It's the only one there sir. His eyes are following the kid into the building. One way or another, that kid is going to pay for what has just happened. I can see the church in the distance but am still not sure of what to do when I get to it. People are streaming in between us both. Must be a bus trip, hey Benny? He looks at me and I smile. He looks at me in the same way he looked at the kid. Am I going to pay later? I wonder.

I make my way down Exchange Avenue, across the widest road I have been on that has not been a motorway, and pass dangling overhead traffic lights and green street signs that send you in three directions: Poplar Ave, Union Ave and B. B. King Blvd. I find the little white church standing all alone, as though it has dropped from the sky like the Tardis.

The church door is locked. I am not religious. I think people believe in God because it makes them feel safe. I don't. Churches fascinate me, especially the cathedrals, because they have been built by humans, literary, brick by brick, stone by stone and it's nice just sitting in them, quiet like. They have a soft hum about them. I've done it a few times more since my mam died. You look lost Elvis?

I turn around and Henry is smiling at me. He is standing up close to me in his green tweed suit. He looks like a leprechaun with a black face. I notice a slight chip in his front tooth. You wanna go inside? He asks stoutly. I tell him, No. I surprise myself. Then why did you try the door? If you wanna go inside you just gotta say so. No, thanks I'm looking for Lauderdale Courts. If you wanna go inside all you need to do is open the door. Henry turns the knob and the door opens. See son it's easy.

He opens the door wider for me to enter but I resist. It looks dark inside and feels cold. No thank you. I really haven't the time. Time, what's that pray? He closes the door. I'm looking for Lauderdale Courts. Never been to Memphis before, have you Elvis? I've been here all my life and some. He steps back, turns and points. It's in that direction but you ain't going to get in. He says, No, it's gated. We are locked out and the rich are locked in. Sorry I say but I don't know why. You don't have to be sorry, he says smiling. It ain't your fault. Come. He turns and moves forward. I hesitate. Come, follow me. I'll be your tour guide. A sudden burst of adrenaline rushes through me. No, it's okay. You wanna see Lauderdale or not? Under my breath I say, but you're a black man and I don't want to fight you. He smiles a cheeky chappie smile, like Norman used to when we was getting ready to rob a gas meter.

You don't want to go home Elvis, and see your mammy and daddy? He laughs and puts his hand into the back pocket of his tweed trousers. I step back and get ready for the plunge. He laughs louder and takes a black and white photograph out of his pocket and shows it me. It is of the King and a young black guy standing together. The King is smiling the young black man isn't. That's me, Henry Fuller. He puts the photograph back into his pocket. He stops laughing and gets serious. See I told you he was my friend. Why you call yourself Elvis, anyways? Hey, man tells me that.

With my body still tense I answer, because it's who I am. We eyeball each other for a few seconds. I'm anticipating the worst. My throat is as dry as a desert. The adrenaline is like an electric current running through my body. But he doesn't move. He stands staring straight into my eyes, as though searching for something. Mine close slightly and so do his. His tone softens and he says, I don't understand man that's all. For a few seconds we stand in silence staring. I drop my eyes and say, sorry, but I don't know why. I never do know why.

I turn and walk back in the direction of the hotel. I know he is following me. I don't seem bothered. Once across the wide road I turn around to see if he is still following me but he's gone. I do a 360 degree turn. I don't see him. A cloud of smoke escapes from a metal grate at the side of the road. I tried the church door and it was definitely locked. I wander back to the hotel and hang around outside.

I Am A Man. What does that mean? I am a man you are a man, everybody can see that. He doesn't have to have it emblazoned across his forehead. A designer cap, I bet. The sun has suddenly got warmer and a green haze hovers momentarily just above the surface of the road.

A group of Elvi's leave the hotel and hang around close to where I am standing. They circle an acned young man with a thinning quiff in his fair hair. He wears turned-up, faded Levis and scruffy black boots. His denim shirt is unbuttoned nearly down to his navel. He looks like he has just stepped out of a fifties cowboy movie. He has a face you think you recognise. He holds aloft a piece of paper.

The Elvi's are gabbling in a foreign language. They look European. I pick out the word Lauderdale. I shout to them No point in going there. It's gated. You can't walk in because it's shut tight. Only them that live in the Courts can get in because they have the number. They look in my direction. I shout, Henry Fuller said so. They all stare at me for a few seconds, prattle in some unrecognisable noise then together turn and walk off down Exchange Avenue. The cowboy growls at me, turns and follows them. I go back into the hotel. Benny is not at the door.

I need a street map because if I'm not careful I'm never going to move out of this hotel and I didn't come all this way to do nothing but hide in here. In the foyer there is a gift shop. It is bulging out with crap memorabilia. The King would have a fit. I find a street map and take it to the elderly lady at the till. Her name is Pat.

She doesn't look at me and tells me it is five dollars. Five Dollars! I shout. I even make myself jump. She looks up at me, Yes sir five dollars. I am quickly trying to work out in my head what that is in pence when a female voice behind me says, what do you want a map for Elvis? Pat screeches like a cat Elvis! The young woman takes it off me, puts it back in the rack and walks me out of the shop.

Why do you need a map? To know where I'm going? Why do you want to know where you're going Elvis? We all need to know where we're going, don't we? I blush it was a crap answer and a lie.

I could stand and stare at her all day. I notice she has a crooked left eye but it doesn't detract from her beauty. But don't you know that already, she says, smiling. How do you know my name? Henry told me. Henry? Yes, and I've been waiting for you. Waiting for me? Yes. I ask her what her name is. It's Priscilla, she says smiling.

My insides go cold. She smiles and nothing is said between us for a few seconds. Instinctively, out of the blue, a gurgled laugh leaves the back of my throat and she smiles the most gorgeous smile again and again.

Faith is taking the first step....Dr King

Henry lies staring at the ceiling with his arms dangling down each side of his small bed. Amelia shouts from the other room, are you getting up Henry or what? I'm contemplating the day, girl. I'm figuring out which way to go. Amelia enters his bedroom and picks up the green tweed suit that is scattered around the room. Now, I don't recall paying you to do that girl. I don't recall you paying me to do anything full stop. They both laugh. She takes what she finds, folds them neatly and puts them on a small wooden chair that sits in the corner opposite Henry's bed.

He props himself up on one arm and watches Amelia glide around the room. You sure can move lady. I have to when you around Henry Fuller. Her slender feet seem not to touch the floor as she moves from one corner of the room to the other. Why don't you stop all that fussing and come and sit down and tell me what you were up to last night with that black fellow from down the road. You know better than that Uncle Henry. I know he ain't no good for you. She smiles down at him then turns and leaves.

From the other room she shouts Happy Birthday old man! He says to himself, There is no need for that girl, a man don't need reminding of that. He shouts after her, I love you Amelia Cole. From the other room Amelia shouts back, I love you too Henry Fuller. Henry falls back into the bed and lies there in the silence.

The pains in his hips are reminding him of his age. He knows if he lies much longer they will get worse, but today he doesn't want to get up. Being seventy-four doesn't please him. Being old doesn't please him, but he's pragmatic enough for it not to bother him. Yet he still doesn't want to get up: happy birthday to me, happy birthday to me. The day's still worth facing, Mae Ray said that at Echol's and Robert's funeral in sixty-eight, such a long time ago. But you're right Mae Ray. I know I'm right sugar.

The ghost of Mae Ray is sitting on the wooden chair in the corner of his room. It's getting harder Mae Ray. He throws the covers off his fragile body and swings his legs so his feet touch the floor. Even though it was one of the hottest nights of the year so far, he slept deep under his sheet. I felt cold. He sits on the edge of the bed, head bent, eyes fixed to the floor with his hands pressed firmly into the mattress.

Henry Fuller, what you waiting for? It's a big step you're telling me to take Mae Ray, a big step. You woke up so you get up that's the deal. He stands up and the pain in his hips radiates down to his feet. He bends his back so his hands dangle. See there brother, you've got movement so move. He stretches to the floor ten times, his hands travel as far as his knees, and he lets out a painful screech its hurting Mae Ray. Course its hurting Henry, you're an old man. With heavy breathing he stands tall and motionless for a few seconds. Now you come to me, she says. He walks to the chair and carefully slips his legs into the green tweed trousers Mae Ray bought him many years ago and leaves the room.

Amelia has set the table for breakfast. Where he sits there is a plate with a pancake on it. In the centre of the pancake is one lit candle. By the pancake she has left a card. He sits down and with difficulty, his eyesight is failing him but he refuses to wear glasses, reads what she has written: Happy birthday Uncle Henry, love you Amelia. He kisses the card blows out the candle and pushes the pancake to one side and sheds a tear or two. I ain't hungry Mae. I understand darling.

A teardrop forms in the corner of his eye. But you gotta try.

The sound of an approaching sanitation truck catches his attention. Henry checks the time via the clock on the wall and slowly gets up from his chair stretches his arms high, puts on his cap and goes outside.

The humidity hits him hard. It's just ten thirty in the morning but already the sun is trying to burn a hole in the back of his head. He walks over to an oak tree by the side of his house that is as old as he is; picks up a trash can that is full to the brim with the week's slops and swings it on to his back. His knees buckle slightly. He carries it to the edge of the road outside his place and waits. He has been doing the same for as long as he can remember and he swears he will never stop. He can feel his heart beating in his chest but he won't put the can to the floor. The truck drives up close.

The man behind the wheel shouts, Happy Birthday Henry. Henry touches the peak of his cap with his free hand, walks to the back of the truck, empties the remnants into its gaping mouth and then drops the trash can to the floor. He is unable to move. He needs to rest a while, catch his breath and get things together.

After a passing few seconds, he sucks in air, lifts the can from the floor, swings it back over his shoulder and walks tall to where the driver sits. You know Henry; we are goin' to have to bury you with that can. Brother, you can bury me in it. It won't matter none to me what you do when I gone.

His shoulder is painful but he won't put the bin down. So what are you boys goin' to do? I don't know Henry. Unions talking about striking but I'm not too sure. You got to do something, brother you can't just sit there and let them walk all over you. I knows that Henry. Henry tells him. Remember sixty-eight? The driver laughs and reminds him that in sixty-eight they had Martin. No sir, it was the other way round, Martin had us. Well, whatever, it was still a long time ago, things have changed. No sir they ain't. Henry points to what is written across the front of his hat. It says *I Am A Man* in bold black letters. The truck pulls away. Henry shouts after it, don't you forget that Jacky Brown. Don't you ever forget what I'm saying. He turns and walks slowly back into his garden with the empty bin dangling from his arm.

His hands and his back are hurting like hell but nobody is going to know that but him and Mae Ray.

Emptying his own trash is something he has always done. Amelia calls him a silly old man. But he tells her it's his connection to the world; his only remaining connection to the world. He is dying but only he and Mae Ray know that. He aims to keep it that way. Not even the doctors know. He knows because Mae Ray told him so.

The long hot day is ahead of him. He takes the plate and cup from the table, empties the cold pancake into the waste bin, takes them to the sink and places them in the bowl. Through his kitchen window he can see Amelia's house. Her little veg garden is looking full. He knows tonight he will get vegetable stew made up mainly of marrow and courgette because it's that time of year, and he has to do something about it.

You got to get out there Henry. I knows that Mae Ray. I ain't ready for you yet, do you hear. Make it soon sister, cos life is starting to crowd in on me.

The house Amelia is in belonged to her mother Winifred. Winifred died a year ago of pancreatic infection. One day she is in her garden getting her vegetable bed ready for the sun, the next she is in her own bed screaming for help, pleading with Henry to see her through. Amelia and Henry were there when she passed over. She ain't passed over Amelia she died. She's with Papa, Henry that's all that matters.

Her papa's name was Echol, Echol Cole. Echol was Henry's friend back in sixty-eight. Echol got killed in the back of a sanitation truck along with his other friend Robert Walker. They were sheltering from the rain. Henry watched the jaws of the truck swallow them up.

Winifred never got married again. Amelia nearly did to Jessie Cooper, a young promising basketball player. But he got shot down on Beale Street by accident back in ninety-two. Sometimes these things happen, is what Henry said to Amelia just after the funeral when Amelia tried to take her own life. Amelia never had a steady boyfriend again.

When his friends Echol and Robert died, Henry lived on the east side of the city. After their death and after the strike that brought Memphis to its knees and witnessed the death of Martin Luther King, he moved across town and set up home close to Winifred and Amelia. It felt right he said. He wanted to watch Amelia grow up he said.

Henry loves Amelia. In sixty-eight, when she was born, he was thirty-three. Then he loved Mae Ray and still does. Now he aches for Amelia and he knows it's wrong. But what do you do with it? It's here and now and he can't do a thing. She says, I love you too Uncle Henry, but it ain't the same. He wishes it was the same. He didn't want it this way but its here and it's hurting.

He moves from his kitchen and makes his way back to his bedroom. On his walls are pictures from the past; pictures that keep reminding him that he is a man. Most of them are from sixty-eight: the battles they fought on Beale Street; the police charging in with their batons and guns raised high. In the corner on the wall close to his bed is the one he had taken with the King.

Henry laughs to himself as he remembers the night before in his taxi with that young pretender. I ought to find him and show him the picture. Let him see me and his boss together, that'll open his eyes. Back in fifty-eight it was, when he and the King were joining the army together. They spoke a few words about Beale Street and Henry made him laugh. He can't remember what he had said but I bet that man would be impressed when I tell him.

How old do you think he was? He weren't a youngster that's for sure. What, about fifty would you say Mae Ray? I would say that's about right. Can you understand a grown man wanting to be somebody else but himself Mae Ray? It happens babe. It's happening all the time. People are finding it hard to face the future in their own skin. Henry takes the picture off the wall, puts it in his trouser pocket, turns and leaves his room.

In February 1968 in Memphis they buried Echol and Robert. Mae Ray accompanied Henry to the funeral. The First Baptist Church on Beale Street, where Ida Wells back in the nineteenth century published the first specific Afro-American newspaper, was packed to the ceiling. There were black faces as far as the eye could see. Not many sanitation workers, mostly relatives and friends.

Robert had no relatives as such, none that anybody knew about anyways. So all Echol's kith and kin got together and decided that they would bury Echol and Robert together. Save on the expense. The city had thrown in some money but it was considered to be more of an insult than a help. So they gave it back. Not everyone agreed but they did it anyways.

Henry and Mae Ray sat at the back of the church with T O Jones a rotund, bald-headed man of about thirty-five. All three sat in silence and listened to the service unfold. Gospel and spiritual were the order for the day. The whole of Beale Street were there to raise the roof and sing their songs. Trade outside had shut down to show their respect.

Henry sat there remembering the last time he was here. Back in 1953 it was. Then he was with his mom and dad. They had just moved up from Shake Rag in Tupelo. His daddy had gotten work in the tyre factory on Hernando. It was in this same church when again he saw the King.

Back in Shake Rag they were kids together playing amongst the long corn. Black and white, it didn't matter none because in Shake Rag they were all poor. None knew each other by name no questions were asked. They would just turn up and fool around then drift back to their own when they felt like it.

The King had sat at the back with some other white boys as was the custom then: black folks up front, white folks at the back. In the white folks' establishments it was the other way round. The King loved the way black people sang the spirituals, sang the gospels. Five years had slipped by since Shake Rag but eye contact showed him that the King still remembered.

Until now that was the last time Henry was in a church. Not that he ever thought he had the faith. No sir, he couldn't get excited about it, not like his mom and poppa could. One night, when he was still living at home, he got in after spending some time on Beale Street sharing a few drinks with Echol and Robert and he said to his pa, a God-fearing man: God does not move in mysterious ways Daddy, cos I don't ever see him do it. No sir, if I don't see it I don't believe it. His daddy turned his back on him and said nothing. He had his back turned right up until the day he died. Henry told Mae Ray that he had meant what he said but it made the travelling through life that much harder.

After the service was over Henry, Mae Ray and TO sat and waited for the rest to leave the church. Winifred, Echol's wife, smiled at Henry as she passed. Winifred was cradling Amelia in her arms. The baby was fast asleep. Mae Ray cried openly at the sight.

Outside, the day was still cold. People hung about the church entrance as though not wanting to leave. The cars with the coffins had left. Henry watched them go and cried inwardly. What's left now Mae Ray? Are you going back to work Henry? TO asked, as they walked down Beale from the church. I might as well TO. Mae

Ray took hold of Henry's arm and gripped it hard all the way in to the Palace Hotel.

In the low-lit bar of the Palace Hotel, dark faces filled the room with their elbows propped up on wobbly tables, smothering glass jars full of beer. They all looked up in unison and watched Henry, Mae Ray and TO walk to the bar. A slow, bluesy jazz number was playing in the background. At the bar the three of them perched themselves on stools. The barman passed Henry and Mae Ray a drink each. What you having TO? Henry asked, a root beer for me Henry. All three took their bottles of root beer and raised them in the memory of Echol and Robert. The rest of the bar did likewise.

So it's happening then boys? TO Wilson answered, Next Monday Mae Ray. We are taking them on, TO says with a smile in his voice. Unless, that is, the mayor gives us what we want. Laughter fills the room, followed by a long silence. We got some big boys coming down from Washington to help smooth the way.

Henry I knows you never voted to strike, says TO, but we ain't got no choice now. Echol's and Robert's death made it so. There's going to be a lot of families out there starving, that's what I'm saying TO that's what I'm, saying, maybe not, Henry, maybe not. TO finishes his drink, slips uncomfortably off his bar stool, straightens up his mourning suit and turns to leave, but not before telling Henry to take care. He leaves the bar.

Henry orders another drink for himself and Mae Ray. This time something a little stronger something he calls a Mae Ray special. You've got to give that man his dues Mae Ray. The union is in his blood Henry a man like TO lives and dies for the cause. I tell you Henry it must be good for the soul to be able to hang your life on something worthwhile. It ain't the day, Mae Ray, for a big debate, that's for sure. Mae Ray smiles, kisses Henry tenderly on the lips, and takes herself over to the small stage where Echol Cole last stood tall and sings a song that melts Henry's heart.

Priscilla holds out her hand for me to take. I take it and it is soft and warm. I hold it a fraction longer than I should do and pull away embarrassed. We both laugh. Are you singing, she asks? I'm supposed to be. She hooks her arm in mine and we walk on. She is wearing the orange slacks and the luminous green top she was wearing last night when she left the hotel with Henry.

We walk on in silence and I am feeling uncomfortable. It's like I'm worrying that someone will see us, like we're walking down a street together back home, like when one of Lorrie's friend saw me with a woman I met at a show I was doing the night before. I am feeling guilty, that's it. Or I feel that it isn't right that a beautiful young woman called Priscilla should be seen walking down Main Street in Memphis on the arm of an aging, dying man with a bad limp.

I want to pull away, but her presence is intoxicating. We are walking along Main like a courting couple and the anxiety is whelming up inside me. I do not know this woman from Adam. She calls herself Priscilla and my name is Elvis and she knows the intimidating black guy that drives taxis and who can open locked church doors without a key.

Priscilla unravels her arm from mine and stops walking. She faces me and asks me what song I will be singing. Love Me, I say. She smiles and says Okay. Straight out and without hesitation I ask her where she is from. Straight out and without hesitation she says, from wherever you want me to be from, loops her arm in my arm and we walk on.

Where are we going? Do you know Elvis my mother would ask me the same question. Priscilla, she'd say, where are you going? And I say to her to see how far it is there and back. We walk on. I want to take in what's around me but my head is in Priscilla. I'm in the place I've wanted to be in since I was a teenager but trapped in a situation that is scary and exciting at the same time.

For all I know this young woman, this attractive, young, sexy woman clutching my arm could be a prostitute or even a killer. She could be lying about her name. She might think I'm lying about mine. She might just be taking the piss or… or, and this is a long shot, she might just fancy me.

Is she turned on by men who look like the King? Or is she just feeling sorry for me? Is it the limp? No, she doesn't know me from Adam yet she acts like she has known me all her life, like she was my daughter or something. Hang on wait… She feels warm against me and that's for true and it feels good. But it's not right. I stop suddenly and pull my arm away. Things are moving too quick.

I look at her and want to say what's going on? Instead I look hard at her and say, do you want to go for a coffee? She smiles and nods her head. I look up and down Main Street with a confused look on my face and suggest the Crown, she says, No Elvis that's going backwards and at this moment in time going backwards is not what it is all about.

So put your left leg in and your left leg out your left leg in and shake it all about. I wish I could. *That's what it's all about.*

It is New Year's Eve when our house was happy.

I say to myself, what is it all about then duck? I shrug my shoulders to indicate I'm lost and confused. She takes my arm again. I gently pull it away and smile. She says, Sorry, and draws her hand back down to her side. For a split second I expect her to walk away and leave me standing here. Instead she says, I know a place on Beale Street, The Palace Hotel. She walks on and leaves me standing. I watch her go.

To the blind man give him glasses to the crippled man give him a crutch it don't cost very much…Mahalia Jackson.

Henry knocks hard and the voice behind the door tells him to enter. The mayor is seated upright behind a fancy mahogany desk. When Henry enters the mayor leans forward spreading his arms across his desk. Behind him on the wall is a painting of an old Southern mansion. He picks up a pen and twiddles it nervously in his hands.

Henry walks to the desk and the mayor beckons him to sit down. Henry refuses and stands as tall as he can. You said sir that your door will always be open. That's right ah… My name is Henry sir, Henry Fuller and it weren't. Henry shuffles slightly. He doesn't like confrontation he never has. Well, son, just a figure of speech. But you're here now boy so… With all due respect Mayor, I am not your son and this meeting ain't going to get far if you keep referring to me as boy. Henry's right leg begins to shake. He is hoping the mayor is blind to his nervousness. I apologise, the mayor says struggling to remember Henry's name. It is

Henry, sir. My name is Henry Fuller and my friends were Echol Cole and Robert Walker.

The mayor leans back in his chair in a way that tells Henry that he don't know shit about nothing. Echol Cole and Robert Walker sir was killed in the back of one of your trucks. I was there. I looked into their dying eyes.

Again the mayor beckons Henry to sit down. Again Henry refuses. This is the first time Henry has stood toe to toe with authority. Oh, there has been the odd scuffle or two with the schools he's been in but he's never confronted anybody that has looked him over like the mayor does now.

The mayor asks him if he is one of the strikers. It is the look behind the eyes. Henry is good at seeing behind the eyes. It is the look of a man that isn't sure of what he has let himself in for and it isn't surprising because the man has only been mayor for two months. He looks to be out of his depth. Henry hesitates before he answers. At this precise moment in time sir my answer has to be no, I ain't on strike. Nor, as you can see, am I at work. Henry is wearing his garbage clothes, torn jacket and oversized baggy leggings. They smell of fish.

The mayor turns slightly in his chair so that his left hand is on the desk and his right hand is resting on the arm of his chair. He begins tapping the desk with his pencil. You know that the strike is illegal, don't you? Yes sir I do but I can't stop thinking about my friends Echol and Robert. You see sir all they were doing was sheltering from the rain, nothing more than that. They knew and everybody knows of the fact that if it rains us Negro fellas don't get paid and are sent home. You pay the white boys that stay in the depot but you don't pay us niggers for doing the same.

Henry is waiting for an answer but it doesn't come. The mayor just leans back in his chair and stares at him. It is a cold angry stare that he recognises and has come across so many times before in his life. But this time he ain't going to say sorry. So you see sir I want you to convince me right here and now why I shouldn't go out on strike, remembering whilst you do, Mr Mayor, that my two friends are dead. Henry's voice is shaking.

The mayor stands up and walks to the front of his desk to where Henry is standing. Henry is surprised at how tall he is and how shabby he looks in his dark, fitted suit. Not befitting a man who runs the Memphis

Corporation and whose family owns a string of laundrettes, he thinks.

The mayor stands as tall as he can with his legs slightly apart. To Henry it looks like the man has grown another six inches at least. The strike is illegal boy. Do you not understand that? It is written in the constitution that corporation workers cannot go on strike. The mayor's close proximity sends the adrenaline rushing round Henry's bloodstream. But he stays transfixed to the spot. Then give the men their union Mr Mayor, and they will all go back to work.

They both stand firm for a few seconds and search each other's faces for a sign of the inevitable. The mayor moves and walks back to where his chair is and flops into it. He turns and faces the wall behind him. You know boy my daddy had a plantation and never at any time did he have any trouble from his Negroes not even a backchat, and you know why Henry? Because we looked after them took care of their needs knew every one of them by their first names. The city has got a lot to answer for.

Henry is left standing staring at the back of the mayor's head. He notices a small bald patch. He has an urge to shout at the man do you know you've got a bald spot just like Robert. And that's the truth Henry. The mayor remains looking at the wall. Take it how you want Henry. You work it out boy. Henry senses there is no more to be said and leaves, leaving the mayor in a world of his own. He closes the door behind him.

Hold fast to dreams for if dreams die life is a broken winged bird that cannot fly……..Langston Hughes.

I can't do no more but follow her. You would call it stalking I suppose. I stay a distance behind, making sure I don't lose sight of her, and with each step I keep saying to myself it's not right it's not right. Turn back you dick, the streets are not paved with gold. But they are, this is Memphis, and I do it all the same. If I didn't expect to feel different here in Memphis, then what did I expect? I don't know is the short answer.

Norman said, Go on, give it a go, it'll do you good. It's a chance of a lifetime, blue. He always called me blue. He loved *Bonanza*. Everybody on the circuit said I was good. My mam said, when I look at you son I see the King. It's like a re-carnation. What, re-carnation milk? I'd say. We would have a laugh about that. We'd laugh together about most things.

I know it's an old cliché 'my dad didn't understand me' but he didn't and who could blame him. We tolerated each other. I didn't turn out the way he wanted. The 1984 strike sort of sealed it. He stayed out. I stayed in and halfway through it, I left. So I had a go and won. Then I won again and again and here I am stalking a woman I don't know down Main Street in Memphis Tennessee.

She turns left onto Beale Street and I follow. I know its Beale Street because I can see the green street sign hanging high in the middle of the road; Beale Street left, South Main straight on. Priscilla stops outside a building called The Palace Hotel. I wouldn't call it run down just old, like it has been standing for a long time. I did read that the city wanted to flatten Beale Street, build houses or something. I know it isn't the same Beale Street that the King would walk up and down but I bet The Palace Hotel was standing here then.

There is a promenade of chairs and tables outside with people sitting at them. Priscilla is seated at one of them. She is leaning forward in her chair with her legs crossed and one arm resting on the back of the chair. She is looking in my direction and smiling. She's so sure of herself. I've ordered you coffee is that okay? I sit down without saying anything and deliberately divert my glance away from her.

I think by doing so it will show that I am relaxed when really I am feeling, inside, like a scared rabbit that is locked in the headlights of an oncoming car. I'm fifty-three years of age and I am dying. I'm fifty-three not a smitten twenty-year-old on his first date, although it feels like it.

I look at her and she is still smiling. It's a smile you see on one of them young women in a chocolate advert, all gratifying. She isn't saying anything and neither am I. I can't, words won't come. I look away and see Henry walking towards us. He is wearing a green tweed suit. He is smiling too. I say out loud, what is all this smiling? I'm drowning in smiles. Priscilla looks at me, leans forward and puts her hand on mine just as Henry arrives at our table. Elvis, my friend, we meet again.

He holds his hand out for me to shake. I shake it reluctantly. His grip is strong and his hand feels rough.

Like my dad's hand felt when he held mine as we watched my mam enter the fire.

People at other tables turn round to look at us. And he says to me, who's this gorgeous young lady Elvis? Priscilla stands up, curtsies and holds her hand out for him to shake and like a love-struck fan, she says, my name is Priscilla and what is your name pray sir? It's Henry Fuller ma'am. Seconds pass before they disengage and it's Henry that pulls away first. Priscilla sits down laughing to herself. I say to them both, I thought you knew each other already. They both ignore me.

Ain't that something folks, we have the King and Queen themselves dining at The Palace Hotel. The people seated around us clap. What you drinking folks? Just coffee, Priscilla says. Why Henry, do you want to join us? Nice of you to ask Priscilla but I've got business inside. He touches his well-worn hat that has you know what written on it (and you would know what if you have been concentrating), bows, smiles and walks into the hotel.

So Elvis, someone else besides me knows you. I'm not going to let this thing drop. I thought you knew him too; last night outside the hotel. Me? She says. Yes, you, I saw you leave and go to him and I watched you walk down the road together arm in arm.

Her demeanour changes, she leans on the back of her chair and looks at me in a way that suggests she is not pleased with the questioning. I don't want her to leave so I change course. I don't know him as such, I say. He drove me and this other guy from the airport last night. It was some big guy who sat next to me, on the plane, coming in from New York. He was going past the hotel to where he lives – a place called Germantown – and offered me a lift in his taxi. We exchanged names. What was his name? She asks. I say, George Montgomery and the driver, Henry, overheard me say that my name is Elvis.

He was also at the church this morning. What church? Oh, you know that white church that stands between the hotel and Lauderdale Courts. You mean the the big brown catholic church. No, I say surprised at her remark. Who was standing there, George? She asks. No, I say Henry. Now she is smiling. Funny really, I tried the door and it was locked. When he tried it, it opened. Who, George? No, Henry. I realise she is teasing me. But at least things are back on course. I got this idea in my head that it would have been a church that the King and his family had gone to. She says, I bet Henry would know. And before I can say anything else she gets up from her chair and walks into the hotel.

A woman looking about as old as I do, dressed in jeans and a white tee-shirt with a young Elvis on the front of it brings two coffees, and puts the bill under the ashtray in the middle of the table. I thank her and she turns and walks away without responding.

I bet she's pissed off by it all. I bet she's one of them locals who just hate this time of the year. I can just imagine her getting home tonight all tired and grumpy, collapsing in a big ugly comfy chair and telling whoever is there, that she had served Elvis and Priscilla and having a good laugh about it. Then again, she might be going home to an empty house and saying the same thing to her cat and still having a good laugh about it. Still, I'm not bothered. Can a man like me afford to be bothered? Like I said, it was my choice and that's what it's all about. I put my left leg in and I'm shaking it all about.

I'm sipping my coffee and beginning to wonder where Priscilla is. I take another sip and wonder some more about Priscilla. I'm toying with the idea of leaving, going back to the hotel and why not? I don't know either of them and I owe them nothing. I wouldn't have put myself in this situation back home. I couldn't have been bothered by it all. I'm on stage tonight, for Christ sake, the Civic Hall, if I can find it – another reason to have gotten a street map. No, back home I would have said fuck off to her and Henry. I wouldn't have even been in his company that's for sure.

It's not that I haven't been around black people, I have. I worked with two in the pit I was at, Ken and Danny. We didn't mix outside of work but we had a laugh when we were on the coalface together. In the canteen they seemed to gravitate towards their own and we did the same. Danny had a nice looking daughter, Jill. She wasn't as dark as Danny, she was mixed race. I went out with Jill a few times but it didn't lead too much. I couldn't take her home to meet my mam and dad because he was against it. He'd say, going out with a half-caste it will only lead to heartache and what about the kid?

We met in the miners' welfare. It turned out she was a big fan of the King, which surprised me. My mam was alright with it but she still said, better not son your dad's right, it's not fair on the kids. I said to them,

Jill done alright. Anyway it just fizzled out. I never went to her house she never came to mine.

I remember one day down the pit we were having our snap and a conversation broke out about immigration. My dad mentioned Enoch Powell. Said the man was okay, knew what he was talking about. It got a bit heated. Then he remembered Danny and Ken was sitting with us and said but I don't mean you two.

Danny couldn't stop laughing and the shop steward told my dad he was a racist. My dad and the shop steward got up onto their feet and squared up to each other, my dad turned to me and said, are you going to let him speak to me like that? And while those two was shuffling round each other Ken got up and said to us all, before walking away: All white people are racist. And some white fellow, I forget his name, shouted after him No we're not, you black bastard, and everybody, to a man, even Ken and Danny, laughed till their bellies ached. I remember somebody was sick. I've never forgotten that.

My watch is suggesting I should make a move. The Civic Hall sounds posh and all legal like. I bet Henry would know where it is. More to the point, Priscilla would know, beautiful Priscilla. Fuck it, fuck it and fuck it, I will bite the bullet and go and ask them. That would be a good enough reason to go in there. I want to be with Priscilla. There seems less people sitting around outside now. The heat feels like a lead weight. I leave the two coffees on the table and make for the hotel.

Our lives begin to end the day we become silent about things that matter....Dr King

The Palace Hotel is filled with less people now than a week ago. The mayor is still refusing to recognise the union and over a thousand workers, all black, are still out on strike. Henry is nursing bourbon at the bar. Mae Ray is on the stage in the corner of the room singing about there being just one more river to cross and one more mountain to climb.

Outside people are stamping their feet harder, clapping their hands louder and shouting the same words to the same song while inside the sweet mellow tone of Mae Ray's voice smoothes out the wrinkles in Henry's brow. While she sings Henry can see the ghost of Echol sitting next to her strumming his guitar.

It was Echol who brought them together. She had wandered onto Beale Street from Natchez, her voice earning her keep along the way. Henry had popped in from the rain to speak to Robert about something and she was standing there, her hair shining black like coal and her brown, soft face beaming like the sun, serenading the heartstrings of the men and women listening. Echol said, this is Mae Ray, and Henry said, yes I know. He never did speak to Robert.

She finishes her song, leaves the stage and sits by Henry at the bar. She lifts a glass of green coloured liquid to her lips, her own concoction, and sips it slowly. She drinks it with her eyes shut looking like she is savouring every drop. Henry watches her with love in his eyes. When she has finished, she slowly and with precision puts her empty glass back down on the bar.

Outside people are marching. We should be out there Henry. Henry leans over and kisses her on her lips. The man never blinked his eyes Mae Ray. What'd you expect? He has a plantation mentality and you ain't ever going to shake him of that. Not sitting in here anyways. At least it's safe. You want safe Henry Fuller? Then why don't you just sit there and let me stick a knife in that big heart of yours cos the only way you going to be safe brother, is when you're like poor old Echol and Robert, dead. That's right Henry d.e.a.d. She is poking Henry in the chest with her index finger while she spells it out.

He playfully grabs the finger and gently and slowly slides it in between his lips. She slowly pulls it away and he lets go. There is silence for a few seconds. He knows she is right.

Henry, my darling, my beautiful, beautiful man, you got to understand. The power they think they got is niggered by our own fear and our own feelings of insecurity, and it's their fear of losing all that power they think they got that moves their hatred for us. They got to blame somebody cos they sure aren't going to blame themselves. No sir they ain't never goin' to do that because they ain't ever had the need to not while they got their version of the Bible and they got the law on their side.

But the feeling of fear has haunted him since he was a child living in Shake Rag. The kids in Shake Rag played together but the grown-ups couldn't, so they all slept with one eye open and with a rifle resting on top of their tanned bellies.

If we are to move on Henry, the circle needs to be broken, for their sakes as well as our own. That is what Martin is trying to do. Henry pours himself and Mae Ray a 'Mae Ray'. Each takes a swallow. Okay Henry Fuller, if you want safe then you comes upstairs with me right now and lay down on my bed. Henry stands up smiling, you and me Mae Ray? Mae Ray playfully pushes him down again. Now, you stay till I've finished. She finishes her drink. Now you coming or what? You mean it Mae Ray? Yes Henry Fuller, I do. I love you woman. Tears are welling up in Henry's eyes. I love you too Henry, but alive not dead. Henry drops his head into Mae Ray's bosom and sobs like a baby.

It is dark. In the background, slow jazz music is playing. I stand, momentarily rooted to the spot until my eyes are adjusted to the drastic change in light. I look around and black faces scatter the room; they are staring at me like they have never seen a white fellow in their bar before. I see Priscilla sitting on a bar stool next to Henry.

I walk slowly towards them and up close I see they are looking at a crumpled up black-and-white photograph that is lying on the bar. I stand between them and when Priscilla sees me she says, Look Elvis, that's Henry. She is pointing at the black man in the picture. I say, Yes, I know.

Henry scoops up the picture from the bar and asks us both if we would like a drink. I say, we have two coffees outside still. And Henry says, not coffee man, something else, something with a kick to it.

Priscilla's eyes light up. I am apprehensive because of what I drank last night and because of what my doctor has said. I ask Henry if he knows where the Civic Hall is. Course I do brother and I'll take you right there when we have had our drink together.

Henry shouts over to the barman and says to him, Sonny, pour us three of your finest – one for me and one for each of my friends here. I can call you that can I Elvis? The barman brings over the drinks and places them in front of us. Henry tells us that we have to drink it down in one.

I should walk away now but I can't. Instead, I ask Henry what the drink is called and watch Priscilla throw it down her throat in one go and laugh. They are called, my young pretender, Mae Ray specials. I look at Henry; I do not like being called a young pretender. Anywhere else, I would have gone for his throat. But I do the same. I throw it down my neck, and it feels hot all the way into my stomach. It tastes like the stuff the doctor ordered.

Ladies and gentlemen the genie has left the bottle.

The inside of my head is spinning. My body is warm right through. Priscilla laughs again, but not Henry. Henry repeats himself; it's a Mae Ray, gets up and leaves. Priscilla, without saying a word, gets up and follows him. It happens so quickly, I just stand and watch them both go. They leave through a green door behind the bar. I stand motionless for I don't know how long and stare at the green door. I flop back down onto the bar stool and put my head into my hand. I am sweating profusely and I have this great desire to go to sleep.

Suddenly the room becomes a lot brighter. I look up and for a brief moment I am on my bed surrounded by four white walls. It is as though somebody has just turned on a light. I shut tight my eyes and open them again. The tables around the room are swarming with Elvi's. No black faces in sight. The table next to where I am sitting is taken by Australians. The women are talking about their recent trip to Graceland. It is like I have been asleep and woke up in a different place.

I remember that we haven't paid for the coffee. I'm looking at the barman to give him the money. He doesn't come. The photo of Henry and the King is still on the bar. I look down at the photograph and the King is smiling up at me. There is a buzzing in my head. It must be because I haven't eaten and I have had that drink. Without thinking twice about it I put the photograph into my trouser pocket, leave the bar and go to the table where our coffees are. I look at the bill and search my pockets for some cash. I find three dollars and put that down under the ashtray with the bill and leave.

Beale Street is bathed in glorious sunshine, full of Elvi's and the King is singing. My body is gently moving to the sounds. Across the road a middle-aged man dressed in an off-white jumpsuit and wearing a green baseball cap is standing beneath the big B.B. King Neon sign that hangs in the sky and he's gyrating badly to the music. Elvi's are crowded round him. They are clapping and singing off-key. Anywhere else and some other time they would not have given the white jumpsuit man the time of day. They would have ignored him and sniggered. They would call him a nutter like they do me.

But this fortnight in Memphis belongs to the King. It's all of us being in it together. It's all of us paying homage. It is me and my mam paying homage all those years back in sixty-eight. Sitting there on the settee they had just finished paying for. The image on the telly smiling back at me, and I bought it. The photograph feels hot against my skin.

I am eleven years old and I have slipped a chocolate bar into my trouser pocket. Mr Hollins, the shopkeeper, wasn't looking. He was serving cigarettes to a man. I didn't go into the shop with the intention of thieving. I didn't do it for a bet or a dare. I just had this impulse to pick it up and hide it and it felt exciting.

I cross the road and walk back on to Main Street. I stand for a minute to try and get my bearings. The King is singing Love Me inside my head. I watch a brightly coloured trolley bus pass me. The black faces at the windows smile at me and I turn left and walk a little quicker than I should be doing, like I'm trying to escape the consequences of my action. Mr Hollins had seen me. He told my dad.

My watch says twelve thirty, mad dogs and Englishmen and all that. I come to 422 South Main Street, a green-framed building standing next to a shop that has Civil Rights Museum written on it. Fatigue is setting in. Sleep is drawing me ever closer. A concrete path at the side of the museum leads down to the Lorraine Motel. I know because there is a big neon sign saying so. Breaking up the path is a stretch of grass. It is neatly cut into a large square and inviting me to rest, perhaps lie down even and stare at the sky. I have read about Lorraine Motel in the blue book.

Miss Jackie Smith says hello and tells me that she once lived right there.

A wreath clutches the balcony that Martin Luther King is lying on sideways down with men dressed neat and tidy in dark suits standing over him pointing to a building opposite. It is a square, brown building with windows: the killer is crouching with the rifle in his hand, job done.

I stand in a big room that has pictures of black people on its green walls. It is morbidly quiet and devoid of people but for Miss Jackie Smith, a fragile looking black woman. She is standing behind a makeshift counter. I smile and she says yes? I say, I would like to go in. She asks me why. I say, I don't know really. She nods her head and points to the sign: 'This way out'. I say, don't I have to pay? And she says, not today Elvis, but you will eventually. I say, how do you know my name? And then I ask her, do you know Henry? She smiles at me and says, everybody knows Henry, and points to the entrance behind. She tells me it's my choice, go inside and find the truth or step back outside and live the lie. I say, what do you mean? She says, in a soft-spoken voice that sounds so much like mothers: I say what I mean and I mean what I say. Did you take the chocolate bar or not? My mam would mock him behind his back.

I just want to be left alone. I am good at what I do and that is good enough for me, see. If you want to go on strike then that's your business. I just want to get up on that stage and sing: From slavery till now is written tall on the green wall. What about me? I know where I am from. I need to be singing my song. I should not have listened to the women outside. I see an exit sign. That is where I should be. Suddenly the lights start to dim and a voice above me tells me I need to be quick; there is no time to wait. On the wall beside me is fourteen-year-old black boy Emmet Till lying dead in a stream thrown in by white men for winking at a fair white southern lady somewhere in Money, Mississippi. I winked at Jill Mace, our teacher in class three, she was forty-three but they didn't hang me. They just told me not to be silly. Edward Tilly, a lad in our school, died on a motor bike playing the fool. The room is dark now.

I stumble and trip and fall against a wall that has a picture of three young, fit men holding dustbins up over their heads and not smiling; the one in the middle is wearing a hat. I feel excruciatingly warm and my eyes close then open again with the sun staring down at my burning face.

I sit up and gather my thoughts. You fell asleep, a voice behind me says. It belongs to Miss Julie Smith, the lady with an axe to grind. She helps me to my feet. I feel inside my pocket and the photograph is still there. I weren't goin' to rob you mister. Sorry, I say. I know sorry and I limp away quickly. She shouts after me, Hey man, what you do to your leg? I wish people wouldn't keep reminding me.

I get onto Main Street and walk back the way I came. The sound of a trolley bus is getting close. My head seems clear now but I am not sure. The King has stopped singing. I turn and see it coming towards me and stick out my hand. It stops and I get on. It costs me two dollars to get where I want to go. The man said, Where to? And I said, I didn't know, so he showed me the way.

I see the Crown ahead of me. I remember it stops there. I see Henry and Priscilla standing close to where I should get off. She has her arm hooked in his. I get off the stop before, hoping they haven't seen me. I want to go back to my room. In an hour I sing my song. I need to change.

I turn left down Union and carry on walking. I look back to see if they have noticed me. I can't be sure. They have left the spot so I stop. I walk on then stop again. I bet Henry is at the Crown waiting for me. He went back to the Palace to retrieve the photograph and found it not there. Next time son put the chocolate bar back.

So what if he is? I'll just give it to him and say, Hello, Henry, I've been looking for you. I'll get in first with the questioning. Hello Henry, what are you doing here?

I soon realise I am lost. I need to be on the other side of the road. There are four lanes to negotiate. Cars are crawling at a ridiculously slow rate but I still have to wait. Down the road are overhead lights so I make for those and wait for the traffic to stop. They stop and I cross.

On the other side, I decide to go straight. I know that the hotel has got to be in that direction. The voice inside tells me so. I walk on some more and a car pulls up. I don't look and carry on walking hoping that it isn't some mugger or somebody asking for directions. It would be the blind leading the blind. Someone shouts, Hey there Elvis.

I don't stop because I think it's some goon taking the piss. It happened in Scarborough once. I was walking along a deserted road like this one and a car passed, slowed down and stopped, just a few hundred yards up. Just like this car is doing now. I could have crossed the road like I should be doing now but I didn't and I don't. I carried on walking. Up close, the passenger door opened. Like this one is doing now. I had a lot of money change in my pocket. I took it out and wrapped in my fist and slid it between my fingers. My dad told me to do that once.

Two lads beat me up. One of them, a Canadian who drove buses, was the boyfriend of the girl I was with. I was fifteen and she kissed like a marshmallow and had just started her period. They painted me black and blue and left me for dead. She said, in my ear, lying there in the road, you are not much of a man are you.

My dad said, Next time son, as if there was ever going to be one over a girl, you must be joking. He said; Make sure you've got some loose change in your pockets. Fifty pence pieces are best son, they've got corners and hurt. Anyway, the bloke in the car in

Scarborough wasn't up for a fight; just a shag. But I hit him anyway. I am not homophobic.

Up close, the voice says, Hey Elvis it's me, how is it hanging? George Montgomery is standing there leaning on his saloon. I walk up to him and apologise for ignoring him. He says, that's okay sir, I understand. You can never be too careful, especially here; especially at this time of the year. I don't want to scare you but it's a fact of life; this is a poor city and there are people out there that will take advantage of that fact if you know what I mean wink, wink, nod, nod. I say, thanks, but I don't mean it.

So you're taking in the sights, he says staring hard into my eyes. His stare disturbs me. It's the stare my old man gave me before he slapped me for taking the chocolate. There are some beautiful old buildings still standing if you know where to look, he says. Have you walked down Main Street yet? I say, Yes, I have. Good, a lot of the buildings on Main are still the old Memphis, you know. You must have seen the Sears building: a beautiful architectural achievement. I say, I don't think so. How, man, did you not notice the Sears? The Sears is Memphis man, like Schwab's on Beale.

They have been open for generations. I didn't tell him I was otherwise occupied I just say, I don't know, sorry.

He walks round to where I am standing and opens the passenger door. You must let me sir, show you the sights. I don't know how to react. He is standing up close. There are sweat marks on his blue linen shirt. The mole on his face seems to have gotten worse. I want to say to him, Hope you don't mind me saying this George, but the mole on your face, my dad had one once and it killed him. Instead I say, that's good of you George, but right now I have got to get to my hotel and change. I've got a song to sing. He screws up his face like a child when it doesn't understand what a grown-up has just said. He then smiles his toothless smile (more teeth are missing for sure) and points a crooked arthritic finger at me and says, Gotcha, okay.

He turns and goes back to the driver's side. You're at the Crown, right? I'll pop by tonight. You look like you could do with some company and I'm your man not them others, if you know what I mean. I just nod my head and give off a weak smile and watch him drive away.

What I want to do right now is to get on the next plane and go home. I do not know who is on the end of the phone, if you know what I mean. I do not know what the fuck is happening here in this city of rock and roll.

I have been in Memphis for a day and it seems that all I'm doing is dodging people and having strange dreams. Last week, or was it the week before, Norm came knocking at my door and told me to enjoy it all. It's where you want to be so make the best of it, sing your heart out Elvis, for me. Poor deluded Norm or is that me.

I look at my watch. I have no time to spare and stare no more. I'm panicking now. What have I got myself into? I turn and walk back the way I came again and again and some more. I'm out of my depth now, I want to go home Norman you prat.

I reach Main Street and see people piling in to a white building with four off-white square pillars at its door. This is it, I'm sure the hotel could arrange it for me, the Civic Hall. I'll say my mam has died and Hank will say, Have you brought a note young Proctor, to prove it's so? I need to get home quickly because my wife has given birth. Is that so Proctor, is that so? Or is it just another lie like the rest you have told? There you are Elvis, there you are. I meant to put it back Dad, honest.

I thought I had lost you. Priscilla is tapping me on my shoulder. I turn and face her and she points her finger at the imposing building opposite. My stomach does a summersault. Where's Henry? I ask her. She puts her arm in mine and we cross the road together and enter the arena through sliding doors.

Hold fast to dreams for when dreams go life is a barren field frozen with snow……Langston Hughes

The Civic Hall is packed to the brim. Henry Fuller is sitting at the back with Mae Ray. The place is a mass of black faces. The only white faces in the room belong to the two New York guys standing on the stage: Wurf and Ciampa. They are the leaders of the A.C.M.E., the union that is representing the sanitation workers in their struggle for union recognition and better living standards. Next to them is seated TO Wilson. He looks proud as punch. It has taken him years to get to this stage.

TO Wilson at one time worked for the sanitation department. He was sacked by them in 1962 for taking a small number of workers out on strike. The strikers were also sacked.

TO Wilson never gave up on them. Every day of their working week he would be outside of the works gates trying to convince his colleagues that the only solution to their problems was to take on the corporation. He can't remember how many times he has been arrested for harassment. Henry Fuller would say to him: Sometimes TO, striking is a luxury that the men just can't afford. They can't spare the time nor the money cos they are working all hours and they ain't got no money.

Henry listens to the speakers telling the congregation that the mayor will not budge. He is adamant that there will be no union in his workplace whilst he is in charge of Memphis. There is hollering and screams of disapproval and shame bounce off the walls. Henry sits quietly. Mae Ray is on her feet hollering and screaming with them. Being like everybody, he thinks, is being nobody

She's pulling at his arm to try and get him to stand, but he won't budge. The outburst of euphoria from everyone around him makes him feel nauseous. He knows that the screams of disapproval and the shouts of shame are for a good reason. He knows in his heart that fighting for what's right like the men and the women and the children are doing here is the only action they can take if they want to feel human, but his head is telling him something else – only what that something else is is something he can't fathom out. There is a great big hole in his heart and he doesn't know how to fill it.

The young man standing on the other side of him looks down on him with a heavy frown. Henry feels the man's anger. The crescendo of noise begins to evaporate. People settle back down into their seats. The man nudges Henry in the ribs. He whispers, you got a problem standing brother? Henry ignores him. Do you want some help in standing brother? He doesn't need to be reminded of the fact.

TO Wilson stands up and speaks. Henry has said to Mae Ray: The thing with TO is he ain't got nothing else in his life. Ever since I've known him Mae Ray, the union thing has got in the way of his living. It has been his number one. And that is wrong because of what, Henry? Asks Mae Ray. It got him the sack, didn't it? He lost his wife because of it. I'm just saying his philosophising has tripped him up too many times. That might be right Henry Fuller, but he keeps getting back up and in my book that's got to stand for something.

Suddenly, without even thinking about it, the image of himself sitting in his car outside the King's gates comes into his head. He saw me there Mae Ray, through the hordes of women hanging around his car, he saw me sitting there and he smiled. Did he come over and say hello? No, Mae Ray he didn't but that don't mean he didn't see. Well there you go Henry. There you go. He smiled because he remembered. I do know that.

TO stands at the mike, tall and proud. He tells everybody that today, beyond doubt, is the happiest day of his life. The auditorium again goes into raptures and again everybody is on their feet; everyone except Henry.

With a wave of his hands, like Moses calling open the Red Sea, TO tells everybody to sit down. You can hear a pin drop then he bellows out: The future is in your hands. We cannot afford to lose this fight. The mayor must not win. This struggle is about dignity; the dignity of every black person living. Every black man living should be screaming in the mayor's ears *I Am A Man. I Am A Man. I Am A Man*. I say to you Mr Mayor, you look me in the eye because I want to say to you. *I Am A Man* I truly am. The auditorium erupts. Every man, woman and child is standing and chanting the words the same four words. *I Am A Man*. Except Henry.

Outside the Civic Hall, the cold air grips the lungs. Police with their hard hats firmly stuck to their heads and their batons gripped tight in their gloved hands are waiting for the people to enter the streets. The voices of the people inside reach them all. There's tension in the policemen's bones. Their bodies wait for trouble. But none comes.

The overjoyed and exuberant crowd of smiling black faces spill into the cold streets quietly and without fuss. They disperse, some going left down Main Street, some going right up Main and some turn the corner and make their way down Front Street, where they will walk past the sidewalk edge with their heads held high and their sensitive noses and mouths covered against the mountain of stench and spillage from unemptied old and battered trash cans that are huddled together like lonely souls, afraid to move.

The people will cross the road slowly and walk on to the banks of the mighty Mississippi and they will sit and discuss the unfolding day's events and sing with both joy and fear squeezing their hearts

We will overcome yes we will overcome.

Henry and Mae Ray, wrapped up tightly in their heavy coats and with the sound of the singing Mississippi teasing their ears, decide to go up Main.

Right up to the Sears building, police are lined on both sides of the road keeping their eyes firmly fixed on the passing folk, hoping, perhaps, that at least one will liven up what for them has been a boring day. One of the young policemen shouts from the ranks, not working today then Mae Ray. Mae Ray shouts back, not today George, too cold. There is laughter in the ranks. It's never stopped you before Mae Ray. Well, you should know, George Montgomery, you should know. The laughter stops suddenly.

Passed Sears, the line of policemen fizzles out. Mae Ray pulls Henry closer. I thought you had done with all that Mae Ray. Mae Ray pulls him even closer. I'm surprised at you Henry Fuller. Nothing more is said on the subject. They make their way along a relatively quiet Main to Beale Street and then onto Mae Ray's home, upstairs at The Palace Hotel.

Once inside the cold, cramped small room with its tiny stove and two rickety wooden chairs, Mae Ray takes off her coat and hangs it on a hook on the back of the door. Henry plonks himself wearily down onto a small well-worn sofa for two that is shoved up close to a tiny oak table that fills the centre of the room.

What you having then Henry, something soft or something hard? Give me coffee. What, you coming down with something? Just coffee Mae Ray, I don't feel like something else. You don't want something hard?

What, you sick? I got bourbon, gin. I said coffee woman. Coffee it is, but don't you blame me brother, if you's awake all night. What you talking about Mae Ray, it ain't yet dinner. I'm just making a point Henry. I was just making a point. And what point would that be missy? The point, Henry, that you don't ever take coffee, ever.

Henry sips at the hot coffee as though he is expecting it to burn his mouth. He is lost in thoughts about Echol and Robert and about the pending struggle. He liked Robert but he loved Echol Cole and he's too scared to fight. People change their minds Mae Ray, that's all I'm saying. Sure they do. Henry puts the hot mug of coffee down onto the table. Mae Ray chastises him for doing so, you trying your best to stain it boy, she says.

He leans back in the chair without saying a word. The day has affected him badly, left him feeling tired and vulnerable and scared: scared of more hurt, scared of struggling to live, scared that his fear will be exposed. He so much wanted to join in, be a part of it all, stomp and clap his hands like all the others but couldn't. Now he just wants to go back to his own place on the east side and wallow in his own self-pity alone. Just now Mae Ray is in the way.

Take your coat off hon, else you won't get the benefit. Not today Mae Ray, got things to do. Henry stands up makes his way to the door. You're not staying? Mae Ray, I said I got things to do. Leave it at that. Concerned Mae Ray asks, See you later then? And without turning round Henry replies with a solemn Maybe, opens the door and leaves.

Mae Ray can hear him walking down the stairs and wonders if she has lost him for good but then smiles and says to herself, It don't matter none if it means he's woken up. *We will overcome.*

Henry wraps himself up tight into his heavy, dirty brown trench coat and walks down Beale and towards the singing Mississippi telling himself I will try and overcome.

We are walking arm in arm through a narrow foyer whose grey walls are covered with photographs of the King in various poses. They are arranged in chronological order. There is none of him looking bloated and lost.

But we don't linger; we walk on, through a green door and into a large, totally white auditorium where in the middle, with a sea of multi-coloured and multi-shaped mumbling Elvi's surrounding it, sits the operating table which has on it men of differing ages, shapes and sizes working like beavers to get the vision into shape. I stand goggled eyed by it all. I have arrived. This is it Mam. This is the place I have always been destined to be.

We are greeted at the door by a matron-type Hattie Jacques lookalike sitting behind a trestle desk with her brown patterned dress, blue-rinsed hair and big red glasses staring at me. She smiles at me and says welcome and asks my name. I tell her Elvis Presley and wait for the expected response. I am not disappointed.

She continues with the same smile like it is stuck on her face but doesn't write my name down on the form. Instead she says, in a polite way, No sir your real name.

Priscilla jumps in and in a polite way tells her that Elvis Presley is my real name. I tell Priscilla, in a polite way, that I can speak for myself. With the smile never leaving the woman's face she says to Priscilla, in a sarcastic tone of voice, and what's your name beautiful lady? No, don't tell me, I bet it is Priscilla. How did you guess?

They are eyeballing each and smiling like two automatons but I can see in the woman's eyes that she thinks we are taking the piss. And I suppose you are married, the woman says without changing the expression on her face one iota. Priscilla replies, without changing her face one iota, Course not. Why would I marry somebody who calls himself Elvis Presley?

Now that takes me aback a little. I say, stumbling over the words and trying to diffuse the situation, look at your sheet and you will see my name. Elvis Presley. My birth certificate says the same. My mam was in love with him. My dad hated him.

They are both looking at me now. Their faces have softened. Priscilla pulls on my arm and smiles. A queue is forming behind us. An Elvi behind me shouts something out in German. The woman behind the desk cannot find my name on the list but hands me a name tag all the same and writes something on a piece of paper, hands it to me and tells me to go down to the front of the stage and give the paper to the man in black. I laugh at the thought of it. The man in black, Norm would have liked that.

I give the man in black the piece of paper. He reads what is on it, smirks a little, looks at me and says, in a polite way of course, Okay buddy what song are you singing for us today? I am still irritated by what Priscilla said to the blue-rinse woman and with rising anger in my voice I say with confidence, my name is Elvis Presley. My name is Elvis Presley. I told the woman at the desk that my name is Elvis Presley. I am angry. I am angry at Priscilla. I am angry at blue-rinse and the man in black. I am angry at the whole fucking world. I am angry with the doctor who turned my world upside down and I am angry at the old man for being him and not who I wanted him to be, whoever that was.

That may be so sir, that may be so, but I cannot let you go up there, calling yourself that. *That!* I scream. You will be saying bollocks to the colonel next. Priscilla shouts, and why not that, if his name is that.

And I scream back at the both of them I am not a *that*, I am Elvis Presley.

The time frame freezes. The man's mouth opens in slow motion. I…t i…s s…e…t i…n s…t…o…n…e. I watch him and Priscilla mouthing at each other and I search frantically for the remote inside my head. I want it to stop, pause and start again in normal time if there is ever such a thing and I hear him say, by them that make the rules.

Show me the rules, Priscilla ask. Show me where it says you cannot perform, on this specific day, under your real name of Elvis Presley. The man in black dismisses Priscilla's request with a wave of the piece of paper.

I wrap my trembling hand around her soft white arm and gently ask her the best I can to leave it. I say it doesn't matter again and again till the ballroom ball above our heads starts spinning and time freezes once again and the old man's dying face is screaming, It doesn't matter it doesn't matter!!! It's the only life you have got son. This is your life you're wasting, throwing it away like stinking garbage overflowing. Your soul is dying, I scream whilst grabbing her arms vice-like this time, shaking them angrily until my world falls in when

Priscilla releases herself from my grip, smiles, turns to walk away and I scream:

Don't treat me like a fool, don't treat me mean and cruel just love me please love me.

Priscilla turns and faces me, kisses me, lingering long on my lips. I watch her leave.

I look at the man in black. He takes my hand and shakes it vigorously. He isn't laughing and neither am I. You are good, mister, he says. I say, Thank you but I already know that. His voice is mellow, his words jumbled, Shame to pass you by. Tell you what buddy go ahead and sing. That's it buddy. Buddy, I'm not your buddy my name is Elvis Presley. Give the band your number, mister, he says. My name is Elvis Presley.

In front of me, a group of young men and women, all looking the same with black quiffed hair and wearing brown and white cowboy shirts and baggy grey trousers under long white coats are winking at me and wiggling their hips. They are holding clipboards and writing things down. Behind them with his hair quiffed the same and dressed in a long green coat with black trousers hiked up to his waist, stands a nervous, petrified-looking young me. It is my first gig.

Don't treat me like a fool, don't treat me mean and cruel love me please love me.

George Montgomery dressed in a police uniform is standing at the back of the room near the green exit door, with blue-rinse hair lady and the man dressed in black. I walk towards them.

The room erupts with applause and he's gone. He said he was going to the Variety Club and she believed him. The Rhythm Rascals were on and she believed him. It was New Year's Eve. She patted the cushion next to her and I sat down. We both sat there in silence waiting for her fantasy to start and my life to fall apart only I didn't know it then how could I, I was fucking twelve years of age.

She put her arm around my shoulders and pulled me close until there was no room between us nothing separating us I felt warm, cosy and at home. In front of us the sexy man, lean and handsome with his chest gleaming with sweat and dressed in a black leather suit, sat on a chair with a guitar fixed to his bent knee. My mam sang his songs. *That's all right mama that's alright with you...* I sang along. Is that alright Mam?

I look down at my watch but can't see the time; my head is spinning inside like I've just stepped off a roundabout doing a hundred miles an hour. My heart is doing the same. Norman is telling me to take deep breaths; I'm telling him to fuck off and I stumble out of the room desperate to get away from prying eyes. A voice behind me shouts: Are you coming back son. I don't answer. Beads of sweat are stinging my forehead. I lean against a cool, stone wall. A black man walks towards me and I go cold inside. My heart feels like it's going to burst. I have nowhere to go and darkness descends.

Darkness cannot drive out darkness only light can do that.....Dr King

I feel a tap, tap, tap on my cheeks. The taps feel cold and so does the ground beneath me. I open my eyes slowly and make out a black face hovering over me. I panic and try to get up but my body is heavy and is pinned to the ground. Hold it fellow. Men are shouting and women screaming. I yell at him to let me go and he tells me to stop squirming like a worm. I stop but the shouting and the screaming doesn't.

What's going on? Settle down, don't make a fuss. I do what he asks. I lie still. Are you going to kill me? Because if you are I don't care, not anymore; I want you to know that. He releases me. He stands up and says, I should be asking you that.

I prop myself up onto one hand and I see that I am lying on grass surrounded by daffodils growing in mud. I take a quick look around me and see that I am in a field somewhere. I don't know where. I get up into a sitting position and take a quick panoramic look of my surrounds. The screaming and the shouting haven't stopped. Behind me is a very wide river. The screaming and the shouting are bursting my ear drums. It feels like I am locked inside a scary movie.

I look up at the man. His boots are covered in mud. Are you going to give me a good kicking, fellow, because, honestly, I do not give a flying fuck. A flying what man? Fuck fuck fuck!! The black man makes a noise like a giggle. Do you think you can get up? Why is it so cold? I ask. He says it's the time of year.

He holds his hand out for me to take. I show my reluctance by falling back onto my elbows. It's a trick, I say. He says, I thought you weren't bothered, and holds out his hand again. I'm not bothered, I say. He pulls his hand back and stands over me just looking. The screaming and the shouting are still going on.

I say, Can you hear that? Because I'm not convinced that the noise I can hear – all the screaming and the shouting – is not inside my head. He holds his hand out again and he says, that is why we should leave.

I take it and ease myself onto my feet. His hand feels rough. Dark days, dark nights, he says. My backside feels wet. I stumble slightly and he grabs me and holds me steady. I apologise and gently release myself. What happened? I don't know fellow. I just found you here dead to the world.

Screaming and hollering that's all I can hear. I feel cold round my arms and rub them fast and hard. He takes his heavy looking trench coat off and hands it to me. I say, No you're okay, and he asks why and I tell him because it's yours. But I ain't cold like you, he says, with anger in his voice. I ain't a fool like you, that's for sure. I ain't like you cos you are out in this weather without wrapping up like me. How long you been there? I hesitate. He stands up tall, puts the coat back on, you don't want to wear a nigger's coat, is that what's wrong? He turns and walks away.

Wait! He stops. He says with a wave of his hand and without looking at me, Look mister I ain't supposed to be talking to you. He's moving further away and I need him up close. I walk after him. What happened? I shout. He looks round and faces me, turns and walks on. I scramble after him like a stray dog.

Are you one of them white boys from up North? The screaming and the shouting are getting louder. I shout after him, Can you hear it or is just me? He stops walking and turns to face me. I catch him up and he moves up close and his breath throws out a fog as he speaks.

I am staring into the eyes of a scared and angry man and without looking away he screams at me behind his hot breath, It's apocalypse up there man, and he points to a distant place behind him. It's war man. Main Street has been turned inside out; it's chaos. Where the fucking hell have you been? The police are spraying everybody and it's turning them blind man. Where have you been?

I'm sure a tear forms in the corner of his eye and he hands me his coat again. He says, don't give no heed to the smell it's only my life gone before me. I take the coat and put it on.

He stares into my eyes with an intensity I've seen him somewhere before and asks, you gonna be okay? I reply, I don't know. It feels warm and heavy and smells of fish and rotting veg. I don't know this place. He turns around and walks away. He climbs up a small incline through long grass and withered daffodils. I catch him up. The bottoms of my trousers are wet from the dew. Look mister, he says, you know and I know this ain't good for us, you and me, especially today with all the shit that's going on. We walk on in silence. I don't know what the hell he is talking about and I don't ask him but I'm scared all the same. He breaks the silence. What's with the limp, anyway? It's mine, I say, from birth. It looks bad fellow. I don't notice it.

I'm frantic so I have to ask him the question, what shit? Man you must have been out a long time. I don't know how you got there but I thought you were dead. For a split second I think I recognise his voice. I take a glance at him while we walk on. He looks to be in his thirties but it's hard to tell. Now the ground is more even and a road lies before us. I recognise his profile. I don't know how I got here either. What shit? I've told you brother, on Main and Beale. You must have been out a long time, that's all I'm saying. What about Main and Beale?

You know Martin's in town, right? You do know that much, right? No, no I don't. Martin who? He stops and stares at me with this quizzical look: Doctor Martin Luther King. Are you from another planet or what? Is that why you were in them bushes like one half of a grown-up Remus and Ramus or has some spaceship dropped you? Come to think of it you sure do sound different; you ain't from round here that's for sure. You might have come down with the white union bosses from up North but you don't sound like them either and fasten the coat up. I do as he says.

Following him I ask what the river is called. He laughs. I recognise the laugh. He says, it is the mighty Mississippi man. Jesus you aren't real. We walk on with me dragging behind muddled and confused. I shout, what's your name? That's for me to know. Am I in Memphis then? It's cold and I'm dressed like I have just spent time under a red hot sky. He walks on. You could be from up North, I suppose, could be one of them sympathisers. Please, I shout. But you know man, you putting yourself in some almighty danger coming to Memphis if you are. Remember them in sixty-four down in Meridian Mississippi?

The grass is sodden and long and I am struggling to walk through it. My feet are like lumps of clay. Police sirens are competing with the screaming and the shouting and getting closer every step we take. I catch up with him. Am I dead? I ask. Our walking gathers pace. You are in hell brother, I can tell you that. It wouldn't surprise me if I was. I've been expecting it.

So are you the devil? He laughs and I walk with him and the road descends, into a cacophony of noise. Like a stairway into hell. The man grabs my arm and

pulls me close. I hesitate slightly, he tugs me harder.
Where are we? I ask. We are on Beale Street, he says,
the quiet end of Beale Street the devil's quarter.

A police car is approaching. He whispers, it's
George Montgomery. We hurry on with him pulling
and me doing my best to keep up. The coat stinks that
much it's making me retch.

We reach a doorway to a café. The man pulls me
into it and we stand rigid. I know that name, I say. Shit!
Shit! Shit! He screams under his breath. I knew it I
knew it. His head is resting on the glass door.

He turns and looks at me with fear in his eyes. I
step back slightly and my back leg drops off the step
and onto the pavement below. The black man tugs at
me again, pulling me back up close. Do you know what
he will do to us if we are caught together? He pulls at
the knob of the door, gently at first, then hammers it
hard when he realises it's locked. Come on Benny! Shit
I shouldn't be here I should be up there. Where? I ask.
Up there man, helping my friends overcome.

Through the glass I see a black man walking
towards us. He unlocks the door and we step inside. Are
you crazy man? Fuller what you doing bringing that
man here; he's white. The man locks the door behind us

and follows us into the back room. Every wall is hospital white the kitchen tops clinically clean. I am standing next to Fuller when the tall lanky black man enters. Henry is you crazy? Henry Fuller, I know that name too. What the hell is happening? They ignore my silent scream.

What you doing down this end anyways? Does Mae Ray know you are here? Henry turns his back on us both. I don't know where Mae Ray is Benny. We got separated when the police let fly. Some Panthers at the back of the march started putting things through shop windows and started the fires. That gave old George Montgomery and his mates a good enough reason to break heads and legs. Yeah, I hear the tall lanky one say.

You up there man? He is looking at me when he says it. I look at Henry for confirmation. Me, I whisper. No man, I was looking for Mae Ray when I came across him lying by the river in some bushes. The lanky one turns and goes to the sink that is up against the wall. He turns on the tap with his elbow. So why the fuck didn't you leave him there man? He is washing his hands when he says it.

Henry doesn't say anything. Benny turns and looks at us both. Drying his hands, he says to me in a gentle sort of way, you gotta leave man. Leave? I croak followed by a horrible length of silence. Where? Where do I go? Back to where you come from man. Benny's voice is raised now. And where is that? I scream. I look at Henry for some help.

Benny's right man, he says, you have gotta leave. Benny, Benny I know that name too. But where, where do I go? Benny moves up close and the adrenaline flows like a gushing sea. I step back and find myself with no space between Benny's sweet smelling breath and me. I need to find… A river of fear rushes through me. I push him back and I scream. I need to find the King.

Is in the altogether, the altogether, naked as the day he was born.

The faint sound of a voice is struggling to break through the torrent of hissing circulating inside my head. My body is hot. I realise it is my own voice struggling to be heard. I open my eyes and hovering over me and hiding the sun behind her is the beautiful face of Priscilla. She is smiling and I feel her warm soft hand beneath my head. It feels safe and reassuring. I try to get up but my head spins and falls back. She says, with a soft and gentle tone in her voice, not yet Elvis, not yet.

She kneels by the side of me and eases me into a sitting position. She pulls me up close to her and rests my head gently on her soft breasts. I sense her heat and hear the slow beat of her heart. There is a smell of body odour radiating from beneath her arms. Her hand gently eases my head upwards. The hissing and the buzzing begin to evaporate as I get close to the position we are aiming for. Once there she releases me from her grip and says, Now, how's that feel? I reluctantly say Fine. I didn't want her to let me go. I felt all cosy wrapped up against her soft white breast.

I watch her get nimbly to her feet. She holds her hand down for me to take, says, what do you reckon? I take her hand, ease myself to my feet and stay motionless for a second or two in order to settle myself.

I have been lying on grass. I can smell the flowers I have been lying amongst. Just like my dream. Only then I was cold and wet from the damp sod and the flowers were dead. Now I smell magnolia. I look behind me and there is the Mississippi. I could be in the same place. How did I get here? One minute I'm in a big room the next… I remember standing leaning against a cold pillar.

Priscilla says, Henry found you and rang me. He followed you from the hall and found you lying in the grass. He rang me. Surprised, I say, rang you. Yes, on my phone. I am flummoxed. He has your number? She smiles and takes hold of my hand. Yes Elvis, now are you okay to walk? I take hold of her hand. It is warm and clammy and soft.

I look around and people are staring at me. I see George Montgomery in the distance dressed in Hawaiian shirt and grey slacks. We walk towards him. I try and hide the act of wiping the sweat from my hand onto my trouser leg, by saying the first thing that comes into my head, why are they all smiling? George says, they're just glad to see you're okay buddy. I told you we look after them that come in to our city. Priscilla and George look at each other and smile. The smile unsettles me. It is a smile that indicates friendship not pain.

I look down at my feet and rest my hands on my knees. I ask how long I was out for. Oh, a couple of minutes at the most, George says. I ease myself up into a straight back position, bending it backwards slightly, in an attempt to get some of the tension out of it. I say, I'm sorry.

Priscilla says, what is it with you Elvis? You seem always to be apologising. They both laugh. Hey man, I told you it's no big deal. She doesn't let go of my hand. I realise we are the same height. Still, I say, it is embarrassing. I never expected anything like this to happen. I am lying through my teeth. I had asked the doctor when, he told me it could happen any time, but you should see your trip out. So does that mean I am close? They don't know everything.

I'm staring at George and an image of a copper in a police car jumps in and out of my head and I pull my hand away from Priscilla's. She frowns then smiles. For the life of me I could not harm her. George says to me, and I flinch when he opens his mouth, Look man, I think you should get yourself checked out. I should take you to see my doctor. He will take care of you and it won't cost you a dime. I stutter because I don't know what to say, he's taken me by surprise. It's happened before, I say. It is something to do with my sugar levels. The heat got to me that is all. Like I say it's happened before. I just need to get back to the hotel and have a lie down.

Not knowing where I am going, I start to walk ahead of them both, anxious to shake the fat man off my tail as the Americans say. I look up and ahead of me I hear a voice shout, Elvis. I stop. The man from the stage is hurriedly walking towards me. He stops walking and he says to me in an excitable voice, Elvis you're through to the next round.

Priscilla and George clap and give off a cheer. They both catch up with me and George whispers, you are good man. He pulls away but his odour stays. Smiling, I shake my head say thanks and walk on. Only Priscilla follows me. The heat is suffocating me. Fatigue overwhelms me. I find myself on Main.

I stand and survey the quiet road. Priscilla stands beside me and does the same. The built-up area suggests it should be noisy but the only noise I can hear is the rattle of the rolling tram car. I become aware of my tee-shirt sticking to me so without saying a word to each other we turn left and walk to the hotel.

Inside my room Priscilla asks if I want coffee. I tell her that I need to be on my own. I don't say to her I need to rest. I need to get my head around what has happened – the dream, the audition, Henry.

She takes my hand and squeezes it, smiles her perfect smile and says, do you want to meet up later? I nod my head and smile pulling my hand away at the same time. About seven, she says. I nod my head in agreement. She says, Okay, in the bar about seven then. She leaves and I look at my watch. It says seven thirty.

I turn on the air conditioning and before I lie down on the bed I turn out my pockets: a few dollar notes and the photograph. I promise myself I will find Henry and give him back the photograph. I lie down and stretch out my legs. My body feels weak and I want to sleep but I cannot. The faces from my dream haunt me, get up close. I try to catch a good look at them but they are in and out moving fast while squeezing out the name Martin Luther King.

To the disappointment of my old man politics is far down my agenda. He wanted me in there fighting the cause. You are going to have to face up to who you really are one day and when that day comes you are going to have to stand and fight. Who, Dad? Fight who? you? He would just look at me with that disappointed look on his face and say, I hope you will be ready. Well I'm not. I'm too tired. I don't want to fight no more.

But I do know that Martin Luther King was assassinated in 1968. It says so in my little blue book. And Lisa Marie was born in 1968 too: the first of February to be precise. What he was doing in Memphis, I do not know. I reach over to my left and take the letter from my mam out of the bedside table drawer.

My dad gave it to me after she died. He said to me, in his cold and calculating way, she died telling me not to give it to you before she'd gone. I wish I had been there. It was the King's fault.

He stood waiting for me to open it but I slipped it into my trouser pocket and walked away. I opened it and read it two days after her funeral. I'm reading it again now.

> Dear Son. Life is slipping by quickly now. Time has passed so no need for regrets. Although, perhaps one still festers still and now I cannot do anything

about it. But you can. You know what it is George. You cannot imagine how it felt when I first heard heartbreak hotel. It was on the day you were born: the beginning of one life and the end of another hey. Well that's how I saw it anyway. It was like a Damascus moment and that glorious night in sixty-eight when you got up from the chair and sang with the King it was the icing on the cake. I was so proud. Your poor dad never understood. I said to him you have Karl Marx we have the King.

The letter slips from my hand and I drift into sleep.

Can't you see it? Can't you feel it? It's all in the air. I can't stand the pressure much longer. Somebody say a prayer..... Nina Simone

The singer is somewhere in the back of my head. Directly above me a dim light flickers behind a brown lampshade hanging from the ceiling. I lie and stare up at it trying to focus on its existence. I must have left the air con on because I feel cold. I turn my head to the left and instead of the window that overlooks Lauderdale Courts there is a wall with wallpaper on it. It has faint red and black lines running down. Brother you can sleep.

I swing round at the sound of the voice and a young black woman is sitting on a chair near a door. I fall back and try to make sense of it all. Henry brought you here. My name is Mae Ray.

I turn to look at the woman sitting on a chair. They were goin' to take you back to the bushes, well Benny wanted to but Henry's conscience got in the way. So Benny comes to look for Mae Ray. How he found her amongst the wreck God only knows.

Henry said you looking for the King? I can only nod my head in reply. You some crazy man or what she asks, giggling quietly I don't know, I say out loud. I stare up at the dim light. Henry said that all youse was sayin' is I can't find the King, I can't find the King.

She isn't mocking me. I can tell by the tone of her voice it is sympathetic. And I am, I say, but I don't know why. Well you won't, she says, cos you aint figured it out. I turn towards her. She is wearing a purple flowered dress. I say, that's a nice dress, but the words have a mind of their own. She smiles and looks down at it and says, Thank you, my Henry bought it me. I watch her stroking it.

I feel my body drifting into sleep. Where am I? I ask. I smell Magnolia. I catch myself saying Priscilla? The King's gone back, Mae Ray says, gone back to Atlanta, you are safe here. Beale Street, Main Street is burning, people are out of control, and battered heads are everywhere. Poor Larry Payne is dead shot by a face unknown so they say. Yes sir you are safe here.

I lie and stare up at the dull bulb hanging from a flimsy thread. I turn on my side to go to sleep and I see Henry's photograph on the floor by the bed, slim fingers reach down and pick it up. There is persistent tapping on wood.

I open my eyes. For a second I think I'm at home and in my own bed and it's my mam tapping on my bedroom door. Outside the sun looks hot. Elvis it's me, the voice says.

I leave the bed. I stumble slightly. My head feels like a lead weight. I stand still. Elvis are you in there? The voice says. Balance restored, I put one foot in front of the other and limp slowly towards the door.

Priscilla is standing there with bouffant hair. She is wearing yellow shorts with turned up edges and a pink flimsy blouse. She glides past me, brushing my shoulder slightly. I was worried about you, she says. I close the door and follow her only to reach the bathroom door. I want to be sick. I make a dash for the sink and vomit blood. This is the first time blood has appeared. I turn on the tap and watch the blood and water stream down the hole. They mix well. My mind goes blank.

Priscilla is sitting on the edge of the bed near the window. I notice that the edge of her shorts has ridden up her legs and are digging into her soft white thighs creating a tiny mound of flesh on both sides. They are where my fingers should be right now. I wipe my mouth hoping there are no spots of red lurking. I sit down on the hard chair opposite. What you done to your hair? I haven't done anything, she says. She is looking out of the window. We should go there today. I say, Henry said it's closed. Without turning round she tells me that I need a shower. Under my breath I say, fuck you too. I get up and go into the bathroom.

The air conditioning is rattling like marbles in a tin can. The bathroom walls are covered with white tiles. It reminds me of the hospital I was in. Mr Proctor you have a malignant tumour inside your prostate that has escaped into the rest of your body and is in the process of eating everything up including, eventually, itself. Just like that, no holds barred. I kid you not. I turn on the shower and sit down on the toilet seat and watch the water spray the basin.

I am thinking about Mae Ray. Her beautiful body wrapped up neatly in that trim purple dress. I remember her name. Remembering names from dreams is something you don't do. Only it didn't feel like a dream. None of them feel like dreams. They are like another life. Silly I know.

I stand and strip off my clothes and step under the water spray without hesitation. I stay motionless and let the water cascade over me. My head is bowed and my eyes are shut tight. Mae Ray is smiling and the theme tune to *Journey into Space* jumps into my head and pushes Mae Ray out. More's the pity.

I am crying. My dad tells me to stop being mardy. The water is hot and hurting my scalp and my dad tells me to stop being a baby. I straighten up and the water spreads itself over my face and the walls. The door rattles. The knob is turning. The door is locked. It's a habit I can't get out of. I wait a few seconds before stepping out.

I wrap a pristine white robe round me and move cautiously to the door. I don't want to slip. That is why you should not lock the door, Lorrie says. I unlock it and wait a second or two. It opens by itself. So I think.

In the distance the King is singing Blue Moon. The room door is open slightly. The air conditioning is still rattling and the water from the shower is covering the bathroom floor and so is my blood. I hurry to turn it off and slip but stay upright. I balance myself on the shower edge. It could have been nasty. All is now quiet. I am standing in pools of water and blood. They say that silence is golden but it isn't for me. Not at the moment, not here and now. I want to hear Priscilla's voice. I want to hear her shouting are you all right. But there is just silence. I leave the bathroom and shut the door. Priscilla has left the room.

I'll have a word with Hank about the air con. I dress quickly and put Henry's photo into my back pocket.

The same two Japanese Elvi's from the day before are sitting at the same table having breakfast. They are both wearing similar tee-shirts to the one I wore yesterday. Mine today is blue with no motif. I'm wearing the same blue Levis. They notice me and wave. They grin then point a finger at their tee-shirts. I nod and smile and turn back into the corridor. I make my way to the stairs and descend. A locked door indicates closure. Why did she go? Who fucking knows? What I know is correct. What I feel is correct. What my body is telling me is correct. What the doctors have said is correct. I have made my mind up.

I am on the first floor reception. I push the door open. I walk in a straight line up to the reception desk through a cacophony of people's chatter. Hank, my air conditioning is rattling like fuck.

He lifts his head up from a jumble of figures and grins showing me a mouth full of pretty pearly white teeth. Can I help you… Elvis? Sorry to bother you… um… Hank, I say for real, but my air conditioning sounds like it's doing its best to hang on to life. He pushes his eyebrows together and says, Life? Yes, Hank, life. It's making a rattling noise not too dissimilar to the noise my old man was making when he was clinging to the edge of the cliff, you know, before he tumbled into hell. He pushes his eyebrows even closer, tilts his head back slightly and says okay and writes it down on a piece of A4 paper. I say Thank you and turn to walk away. What room are you in… Elvis. I turn back and say, Sorry… um… Hank but I don't know and oh, I forgot to say there is a pool of blood on the bathroom floor. A large pool of blood in fact so be careful you don't slip. He smiles his sarcastic pearly smile and continues writing something down on the same piece of paper.

I leave the building only to be met by a wall of suffocating heat. I turn left and walk down Main.

Elvi's are loitering, congregating on every street corner; swarms of them cluster like bees buzzing in unison honouring his name. When I see Henry I shall say sorry. But why should I say sorry? I didn't pick up the photo to keep. No son a dare, was it? Like the chocolate bar and the gas meters a bit of fun.

Across the road is the Sears. A department store it looks to be. Art Deco, I think, tall and majestic and green in colour. A building the King would have passed many times. Perhaps even gone in when he had cash in his pocket. By its appearance it doesn't seem to be the type of building that would offer a shopping experience the Lauderdale Courts residence could share.

Where is Priscilla? Why did she leave so abruptly? And why was she looking so different from the way she looked before? And when was that because I'm not too sure? I need answers and I need to have something to eat. I need time. I see Henry in my mind's eye: the Henry in the photograph; the Henry in my dream.

I cross the road and walk down by the Civic Hall. At the road's end I find myself on Front Street. Across the road and down a bank of grass and wild flowers is the Mississippi; the Mississippi where Tom Sawyer and Huckleberry Finn spent their days meandering. It is no River Trent that's for sure. *Tom! Tom!* Tom Sawyer painting the picket fence, the opening lines of my favourite book picket line, miners' strike, eighty-four, and my dad disgusted with me for refusing to strike and at me joining the scabs. Only my money was coming in. I kept reminding him over and over again about that, you'll eat the food I buy and bring in I tell him over and over again.

He grabs me by the throat and pushes me up against the door he has just painted green and whispers close to my ear, ever seen somebody crying for mercy, hey? *Bang! Bang!* They hit the floor like a bag of tatoes; your knuckles are ripped but it doesn't matter cos you're feeling good inside. *Bang! Bang! Bang!* Your whole body moving fuelled by hate, there's no escape you're hooked, violence everywhere, the night oozing blood screaming bodies heaving heads cracking, legs flying in all directions one last moan before the long sleep. What's your game pal. What's your game?

Which side you on, boy which side are you on?

My mam jumps in between. Her screams get louder and louder, you what you what!! And he hits her instead of me so I grab him by the throat and push him away for good. I had the King he had nowt. Then she died unfulfilled: just me and him. So I became Elvis Presley officially. George Proctor disappeared for good.

Gone with the stroke of a pen and so did Lorrie and the kids.

I walk through grass where people of different colour and race loll, taking in the sun just sitting and chatting and laughing; a sight for sore eyes my mam would say, people seemingly happy with their lot. The sun can do that, make people happy: An illusion, no doubt, like life itself; one great fucking illusion so I have been told.

I've not been here before yet it all looks familiar. I walk onto a cobbled road. Cobbles I have not seen for a long time, one hundred that's my claim to fame one hundred marbles scored on the cobbled street where I lived. I was playing Chrissy Croft, with finger crooked I hooked the marble at least fifty yards straight into the hole we had made by removing a cobble from the road on a hot summer's day. I can still smell the tar that held the cobbles together; easy peasy nice and easy.

It says Beale Street but it's not the Beale Street not the Beale Street I was on yesterday; boarded up shops and one open café that is all there is today there is no one about on this Beale Street; silence but for a singing siren of a police car I see in the distance.

I enter the café through a green tarnished door. A bell rings. I gently shut the door and the bell stops ringing. I choose a table with a red Formica top that is close to the door I have just opened and shut and sit down on a wobbly chair that has a red Formica seat; it makes a noise on the yellow lino flooring when I drag it towards me. I pick up a sheet of paper from the table that has written on it a menu: grits, eggs and coffee. Grits what the hell is that. *Yes*.

Someone is standing by the side of me. I turn and look up. He is a tall, lean, bald and black. Where the hell did he come from? I smile, nod and say hi he nods and says how you doin'. His fingers are bent – arthritis like my dad's and George. You over for the show, he asks. You look like you might be singing.

I try to smile but it comes out funny so I drop my head and look at the menu, Can I have a couple of eggs on toast and coffee please? You can have eggs over easy or eggs sunny side up? I say, I don't know what does that mean? He laughs. Are you happy or are you sad? I tell him sunny side up only because it sounds better. He calls me his man.

The tall black man leaves and goes into the kitchen. I'm the only one in the café, I hear a pan sizzling. On the bright yellow walls are pictures of B.B.King, Ike Turner and a guy called Rufus Thomas Walking the Dog and Crudup is singing That's Alright Mama as loud as you like. Is the tall man trying to tell me something? If he is, I agree. I've always thought Crudup's version the best. It's quiet on the street outside the window I am sitting at. The tall man comes back with the eggs and coffee. There you go man. He puts them down on the table in front of me. He just comes out with it.

You know Henry Fuller? I haven't started eating. I look up at him staring down at me. He's wiping his hands on a blue cloth that he has taken from his waistband and smiling. I try and smile back. I don't know him as such? We met yesterday. That's right buddy yesterday and he turns and walks away.

Two black youngsters pass the window holding hands. They are wearing identical blue bomber jackets and she has very short cropped brown hair. I watch them go by. On the back of the young man's and girls jacket is written the words *I Am A Man.* I don't understand. I finish my sunny side up eggs. I don't understand I don't understand. I forgot to take my sickness pill.

The tall man comes out of the kitchen and walks towards me still wiping his hands on the blue cloth. Ike Turner is singing Rocket 88. The tall man is up close. I've just finished my eggs he sits down opposite me. Some say that it was this song that kicked it all off, he says. He drags a chair from under a table close by and rests his left leg on it. I put my knife and fork together in the middle of the plate and gently push it away to the centre of the table.

So why do you think the King (said sarcastically) never got to England? He got to Scotland but never got to England why do you think that is? Presley it's a Scottish name, right? The name Elvis it's common round these parts. I got two cousins with the name Elvis and they been around a long time. Their pappy before them was an Elvis too Prestwick airport, right? He just got off and walked around so I hear, just walked around the airport like he was something special yet around these parts… a stopover, right? On the way back here from Germany when he was in the army, right? Yes sir old Henry knew him in the army, yes sir. He spent some time there did Henry. So he says. Old Henry, you never can tell. Still it don't matter none. Prestwick, hey, he just got out the plane and walked around and he never sang. Who'd believe it? Prestwick, ah strange name and that's in Scotland, right? Yes sir, Prestwick; strange name. He just got on the plane and came right back right back right to good ole Memphis 1960, right?

We both turn our heads simultaneously and look out of the window together and watch a group of black people gathering together on the grass verge near the river. The two I saw pass earlier are amongst them and so is Henry.

Henry is holding a banner. It has something written on it but I cannot see what it says. My eyesight has diminished over the last couple of months. The consultant said it could happen but I won't go blind. Are you sure? I asked. I sat there in front of him alone, sweating. I'm on my own, see. I laughed, more a strange giggle at what I had just said. I see. All I could see, through my mind's eye, was me sitting in my house, the house I grew up in. The house my mam and dad died in too terrified to move. How do you know I knew Henry?

We are looking at each other across the table. Ike Turner has stopped singing. The tall man takes hold of my empty plate and picks it up. Smiling, he leans into me. Everybody knows Henry man. You enjoyed the eggs, right? I noticed he has a tiny scar down his left cheek. Just like the man in my dream. He rises and leaves the table. I watch him walk into the kitchen.

The King is singing

That's alright mama that's alright with chews.

On the bank of the mighty river more black people are getting together. I see Henry in the middle of them still holding up his banner. There is no music now; no noise from the kitchen, the only sound is coming from the air conditioning above the door. It's rattling like mad like marbles in a tin can. Time passes.

I get up and go to the kitchen. The entrance is covered by streams of different coloured plastic strips. My auntie had some at her back door. She said it kept the flies out and more. But she wouldn't say what. I separate the plastics strips and peek in. God knows what I will say or do if he is there. But he isn't. The kitchen is empty and it looks spotlessly clean. Not a thing out of place and everything seemingly in its right place as my mam would say often enough. In fact, it looks like nobody has done any work: the dream kitchen with its pure white walls.

There is a door opposite. I stand up straight with the intention of leaving when it opens and in walks a woman: a plump, short old black lady. She is wearing a purple dress with frills along the hem. She has a green bandana covering her head. She isn't wearing shoes. There is no look of surprise on her face when she sees me, unlike mine.

Standing on the spot and with a calm voice she says, there are no gas meters here young man. I feel myself looking guilty. The word No stumbles out. She moves into the kitchen. Then why are you standing at my kitchen door? I wanted to pay for… your kitchen door? You want to pay for my kitchen door? What you saying man?

She moves to the sink and turns on the tap. No you said my kitchen door. Yes son, my kitchen door, my kitchen, my café. She turns on the tap with her elbow. She is washing her hands whilst she speaks.

I'm sorry, I say. Sorry for what? She says. I say, I don't know why I am sorry. I never know why I am sorry. I just had this urge to look in but I don't know why. She gives out a raucous laugh, turns off the tap and takes a blue towel that is hanging on a peg on the wall next to her. She wipes her hands on the towel and hangs it back on the peg when she's finished. You had an urge hey, you take care of that urge man, I can't remember the last time I had an urge, and she laughs uncontrollably.

Okay mister, you want something to eat? No I've just eaten. She's hushing me back into the dining area whilst she speaks. Then why are you here? And how did you get in? I walked in and like I said I've just eaten. Jesus man, I gone done it again, she says. A tall thin man served me. I gone and forget to lock the door when I left. And what did you have, you here for the King? You look like you might be here for the King. Eggs, I had eggs sunny side up I think. I'm standing awkwardly not knowing what to do with my hands. Well, he ain't here not today anyway.

She goes over to the phone on the wall and takes off the receiver and dials a number. Hey Henry, how you doin'? I got that guy here; you know the one looking for the King. Yes sir. She is looking me up and down. Okay will do. She puts back the receiver and beckons me to sit down. I sit down, turn and look out the window.

The street and the grassy areas are covered with dancing and singing Elvi's. Look at them all, the old lady says, same place same time don't they look pretty all dancing and singing same time same place. I do wish though sometimes they would throw some of it my way. It is what it's all about at the end of the day.

Putting your left leg in and shaking it all about.

Don't you think? I just wish they throw some at me sometimes. Yes sir, I sure would be grateful. So Elvis, you and the King what is it all about? And she is smiling like Miff smiled when she caught me singing.

Miff was the old lady who lived next door to us on our cobbled street just like this one. She was a widow. Bert her old man got killed coming out of the Old Rose, a pub near where we lived. He got trampled on by two shire horses pulling a barrow-load of empty beer barrels. They were turning to go into the brewery yard next to the pub. It was Bert who got me dad down the pit.

Miff took care of me when Mam and Dad were at work. I called her Miff because at an early age I couldn't say Smith. The name Miff stuck. The last time I saw her she was standing on her front doorstep at her home on the street where we lived before I moved back. She had shrivelled up. I wanted to tell her about Lorrie. She liked Lorrie. I smiled but she didn't smile back. She didn't know who I was. She got agitated and shouted, no screamed at me to go away. I don't know you I don't know you, she said. I walked away and I cried. I loved Miff. She had gone when I had moved back home. The Slater's live there now. I don't know them from Adam. I didn't cry at my mam and dad's funeral, or even when Lorrie left with the kids. He served me the eggs sunny side up.

There is a knock on the door. I turn round and see Henry standing there. The lady gets up and goes over to the door and unlocks it with a bunch of keys she takes out of her skirt pocket. Henry steps in. He is wearing the green tweed suit. He walks over to me. He takes a chair from another table and sits down next to me. He says, so you are still looking for the King? The lady comes back and sits down and folds her arms across her chest. I didn't forget to lock it, she says. It's starting to feel like an interrogation with them both in front of me. But you've been caught lad, you and your mate here, robbing the meters.

Having breakfast Henry, sunny side up, she says. Henry leans forward and puts his left hand on my right shoulder. Where's my photo Elvis? I'm sorry; we're sorry, aren't we Norm? It was a bit of fun at first. Then Henry leans back and in a less serious voice says, it doesn't matter none.

You left it on the bar in that place on Beale Street yesterday and I picked it up. I can feel myself getting angry; if this doesn't stop soon I am going to hit somebody. Fuck the consequences, I'm dying anyway. It's what I do, ask Lorrie, if you can find her that is. Or ask the kids if you can find them too. In front of me are sitting two old people, not the two coppers who gave me and Norm a slap for wasting their time.

I say, I don't understand this. Understand what Elvis? Henry asks, This Henry, this. And I stand up. I look at them for some reaction. There is nothing to understand, the woman says. We just want to help find your King, that's all. They look at each other, smile and lean back on their chairs. This is Memphis after all. Anything can happen here. Are you singing today? I'm supposed to be. You're supposed to be? I don't know is the quick answer. I'm sorry. I slowly move to the back of the chair I am sitting on.

Mae Ray here she knew your King. She worked for him, isn't that right Mae Ray? I look at Mae Ray and she smiles. She is the lady on the chair. But she is not, she looks different. Yes sir, I did. Mae Ray used to let me in the back when the King wasn't in, isn't that right Mae Ray? I stand, push the chair back turn and walk to the door. We used to play, didn't we Mae Ray? Henry says, smiling. What do you mean I suppose? You either is or you ain't.

I stop, turn and face them. I say, He had a scar down his left cheek and I got a feeling I had seen him before. Who, ole Benny you mean? No ole Benny's gone, if you know what I mean wink, wink, nod, nod. They both smile and wish me a good day. I turn and open the door. I slip my hand into my pocket and the photo feels hot.

Empty your pockets young man, let's see what you got. It's my photograph it's my history not yours. I shout back I'm sorry and leave. The heat hits me hard. I'm starting to feel like I've been swimming in circles. Everything is sticking to me like glue and my stomach feels like it's ready to spew. Nothing is in sync anymore.

I struggle up the small incline to a crossroads: Beale Street straight on Front Street left and right. They warned me not to come. Lorrie called me an idiot. She said you won't get insurance and I said I won't tell if you don't. She called me selfish; she said I've always been selfish, always putting myself first. Who knows where the kids are.

I stop on the corner of Front and Beale. I wipe my forehead with the handkerchief from my pocket. You look lost Elvis. I turn my head to where I think the voice is coming from and I see the fat man sitting in an old white Chevrolet with his head out of the window. This is all I need. He waves me over with his left hand.

I take reluctant steps to where he is. I'm standing next to his car looking down at him and he asks me to get in. No thanks I am going to sing. When? I'm looking at my watch trying frantically to say something coherent. I say Soon. But you want to find the King, don't you? He has a smile on his face when he says it. So let me show you where you might find him. The offer is compelling. But the fat man literally gives me the creeps.

You been to Graceland yet? He says, grinning like a Cheshire cat waiting for its feed. No. Then hop in and I'll take you there. I look at my watch again. I want to see Graceland there is no doubt about that. But this man… I go to the passenger side and get in. I need to throw up. I need to stop at the hotel first and pick something up, I tell him. He does a U-turn. Your wish is my command, and goes back up Front then onto Main.

He stops on Main and points out to me the Orpheum Theatre. See that building there. The Orpheum you mean? Your man sang there but I think he's gone. He turns his body some more to the right and points to the opposite corner. Have you heard of the Lansky brothers? And I say yes. Well that's where their shop would have been when your emperor shopped for new clothes.

You wouldn't see any white faces around here at that time. No sir, this is where the niggers came to play. This was their place, if you get what I mean. Beale Street belonged to them.

Your man was an exception though, him and Dewey Phillips. They said he sounded like one of their own so they welcomed him in to their sanctuary. They said he was okay. Sam Phillips introduced him to Dewey. Dewey was a disc jockey over in the Chisca Hotel in a studio called the WHBQ, it was there he played your man's first record. You heard of Sam Phillips I presume? Yes, I say, wishing he would make a move. Well, old Sam he was recording niggers at the time your man came along. I'm fidgeting in my seat. That word nigger is eating into my brain.

Sambo, that's another one. My dad got pulled over the coals for using that word. A black guy down the pit, one of the gangers it was. My dad called him that word. Pass me the hammer Sambo please. I was standing next to him when he said it. Ken his name was. He passed him the hammer without saying a word, until later. Ken had taken offence to that word. Ken reported my dad to the foreman for using that word. My dad couldn't understand it. Neither could the other white men. Neither could I. He said he meant nothing by it. My dad was a socialist and proud of it. They had been mates for years him and Ken but we still didn't get it. My dad wouldn't apologise for using it. Ken never spoke to him again. Ken wanted my dad disciplined; he wanted the union to discipline him too. They didn't, they said that my dad wasn't a racist and it had been a misunderstanding, after all it was just a word they said. Ken, at the meeting, shouted out that all white people are racist. But I've told you that before. The union suspended Ken instead for insubordination. But that was a long time ago.

I know I'm one. That fact is true. But that's the first step, so they say, recognising who you are and what you are. Like an alcoholic told me, once you see the truth in it, admit it, then you can change. If you want to that is. Ken said some people don't want to change because they find comfort in it. I said to him, Do you? He never spoke to my dad again or me. But nigger just doesn't sound nice, does it? Not anymore it don't. We straighten up and drive on. Did you know I use to be a cop? The fat man says.

 It's not long before we are on Highway 51. There's nothing to see till we get close to the big iron gates where lots of people are milling and writing things on the already disfigured wall. People, in colourful memorabilia, hand over money and get on a small bus with the King's smiling face stuck to it.

 I was at the funeral in seventy-seven, he says. That was certainly a barmy day. I stood over there at that wall close to the gates. Man it was scary. Thousands of people ready to explode, if you get what I mean. I say, did you get a look in the funeral car? Yes sir I did and he was smiling cos he knew me and I knew him. When it came out from behind those gates men and women were screaming in agony. He pulls away and goes further up the boulevard. He smiled at me and said things will be okay now. I know all the nooks and crannies of this place, he says. He's bound to be in one of them.

We turn left and then right, right and left again onto a tiny dirt track. We bobble a bit further on then stop. We've come to what looks like an orchard, with strange green fruit hanging from the trees. I say, the fruit. He just nods and tells me to stop worrying. You will be there soon, he says. The picture looks bleak.

I would have no trouble in taking the guy on despite the alien inside me crawling and eating my innards. I will make sure of that. He turns off the engine, opens his door and steps out of the car. I sit here thinking; I'll jump into the driver's seat and drive off. But he hasn't left the keys in the ignition. I watch him go round to the back of the car to the sound of clap clap clapping hands. Now it's quiet again and the stillness goes on forever.

It's quiet. I slip down my seat and curl up like I'm ready to pop out of my mam's womb and wait. My heart is going ten to the dozen. I do not know what to do. It's late and how long I wait for I cannot say. Eventually I slowly ease myself back up into a sitting position. I expect to see faces peering through the window: a deliverance sort of moment, you might say. No one is there. Time passes.

I'm sitting, struggling to keep myself positioned, waiting for him to reappear. He doesn't. I get out of the car slowly, anticipating a shot through the head. I don't mind saying I am scared. The pain in my side is getting worse. Where did that come from and what is going to happen next I wonder?

Outside the motor I cautiously straighten up and then, when I realise no damage has been done, I move slowly to the back of the car. I imagine him lying there with a bullet through the back of his head. But he's not because he has gone, disappeared. What the hell. I look around me for any sign of movement but there isn't any. What is happening?

Yesterday, or was it the night before, when Priscilla came knocking at my door? I don't know, I can't remember. I walked into the hotel and went to sleep, got up, stepped out. The fainting I understand, it goes with the package, a package deal if you like. But the other things, the dreams perhaps, I can't. Priscilla, Henry, the ex-copper what's his name I've forgot, Benny and Mae Ray, and the sunny side up eggs and

Mae Ray who I have seen before, but not in the same way.

I drop to my knees and, doing my best in the circumstances, I look under the car. Who knows? I get up, turn and face the orchard; the green strange fruit is dropping from the trees. I face the way we came. What was the clapping of hands sound I heard? I attentively walk on but nothing is looking familiar. I have not yet come to the left turn that we took.

Everything now around me resembles a wood. It's like the wood we have close to where I live – the Dumbles we call it. On the days I felt good I would take a walk there. There is a clearing in the Dumbles that is perfectly still and quiet. No birds, no rustling of trees, no noise from traffic on the road that runs parallel to it. It is perfect and I would sit on the grass and listen to the silence. I'd sit for hours and just listen and let time pass.

There is no sound now, here in this wood where I'm half expecting the fat man to come rolling up behind me sweating and breathing heavy and saying, where you going man, what you doing here, don't you know you're trespassing? I'm a coward at heart. The old man was right.

Clap! Clap! Clap! Sends me running for my life and the clapping won't stop. My gammy leg lets me down and I trip and stumble but keep on running until my head starts spinning and everything stops. I fall. I open my eyes and the sun has gone and I feel cold. I'm wearing just a white tee-shirt. My arms are freezing. I ease myself up into a sitting position and rub each arm vigorously. My head feels woozy; all around me small ash and elm trees block out the dying light; under me are dead leaves. Are you okay?

I jump to my feet and turn round quickly. My leg lets me down again and I stumble and fall onto one knee. The voice holds me under one arm. There. It helps me to my feet and stands with me holding me round my waist. You okay? I will be. I straighten and turn. You've hurt your leg. No, I say it's just shorter than the other one.

She's young, about thirty, and wearing a blue fleece coat and tight black Levi jeans that are tucked into brown suede booties. Her head is covered with a Memphis Steelers baseball hat and she has long sticks tucked under her arm. I say, Thank you. What was the clapping? I ask her. She nods her head and says: You must be freezing. How long you been down here man? I don't know. I study her face and I say, have I seen you before, Priscilla? Priscilla? She laughs and steps back from me. Do you think so? I'm not sure. Priscilla is a beautiful lady. No it is her day off. She laughs some more and steps back some more.

Anyways what you doing here dressed like that? I'm looking for the King I think. Me too, she says and laughs again. We look at each other and smile. She walks on. She is of a mixed race. So, how long have you known about this place?

I follow her. I don't,I say. You're telling me you just stumbled on it, right. That's right. You honestly don't know where you are? She stops and turns to face me. No, honestly, I honestly don't know where I am. A man, George Montgomery I think, yes that's his name, wanted to show me Graceland and I landed up here. So he dumped you here and left you for dead? You took a beating, right? I don't think so. You surprise me. Why's that? Cos ole George he takes pleasure from it. You know him? Everybody knows ole George. She gets up close and examines my face. I don't see any marks on you. No. She walks on and I follow.

She laughs and says, you talk funny you're not from round here. No, I'm from up north. Where about from up north? I tell her Nottingham. I couldn't think of anything else to say. Nottingham, never heard of it. Near Birmingham you've heard of Birmingham? Alabama, sure I have. The night is drawing in.

We walk on some through dying bramble bushes that catch the bottom of my trousers and they rip. We walk on in silence but for the noise of rotting plantation beneath our feet making a squishing and a crunching sound. Where are we? I ask. This, my friend, is Grace's land. She is our friend and I collect sticks. Oh, what for? For my grandma's fire of course, she says. Can't let it go out. In the summer I collect apples and pears and take them to her. Can't let her starve, can we. We come to an opening that backs on to a dirt track. Who is Grace? I ask.

On the other side of the track is a neatly painted, two-tone brown wooden bungalow standing alone. I ask her why it is so cold. She says it always is this time of the year. A light is on inside. There are two doors each side of two lace-covered windows sitting side by side and a high wire fence surrounding it all and a well-kept lawn: Granny Proctor's house it looks like. The young woman crosses the track. I stay where I am.

She stops on the other side and beckons me over. I am not sure about this. But what is the alternative? I don't know where the hell I am and it's cold. She beckons me some more, gets fed up of waiting, turns and walks through a gap in the fence and up to some wooden steps that lead to one of the doors. The left one it looks like. She turns around again and looks across at me as though giving me another chance. I don't move and shout, who is or was Grace? I watch her climb the steps and enter the house through the green door. She closes it behind her.

*I am moving into a land of both shadow and substance
...Rod Serling*

There is silence again. I can see shadowy movements behind the lace curtains. The wind is getting up and disturbing the trees. Surprisingly, I do not feel scared. I don't know where I am but I do not feel scared. Grandma Proctor what beautiful eyes you have got. Follow me said the spider to the fly. She was a nice spider, a spider woman that reminded me of Priscilla but I don't know why.

I hear a police siren screaming. It is getting closer. I step back onto the edge of the wood. A police car slows down as it gets close to where I am standing. Perhaps it is looking for me. I make a move to step into view when a man's voice bellows from the car:

Wee Willy Winky runs through the town, uptown and downtown in his nightgown.

Another male voice, louder than the first and an octave higher, joins in.

Tapping at the windows and crying through the locks are all the nigger people in their beds because it's past eight o'clock.

The light in the house has gone out. Forgetting how cold I am I turn and step back into the wood. I hide behind a tree and make sure the house and the car are still in my sights.

One of the policemen gets out. He flashes his torch in my direction. The beam catches my eyes. I make a sudden jerk to get further round the tree. I can hear dead leaves crunching and the noise is getting louder and seemingly closer. I should be scared witless but I'm not. So if he finds me at least I'm white and soon to be a dead white at that.

Suddenly *Clap! Clap! Clap!* And I freeze. He's firing his gun at me. Now I'm dead for certain, one way or another, who cares. It is at this point in the dream where I wake up but I don't. I suppose death has to be experienced first; whatever that means.

I stick my hands up in the air, close my eyes and move to the other side of the tree to receive the inevitable; whatever that is. There is silence instead for a very long time it seems. I open my eyes slowly and somebody screams in my face BOO! My gammy leg lets me down again and I stumble backwards still with my hands in the air and my eyes tightly shut. Go on shoot, you bastards! I scream. I'm dead anyway.

There is silence. I open my eyes and towering over me is the mixed-race girl minus sticks. She says, Man, you're strange. Me? I say, me strange? With her help I struggle to my feet. Did you not hear that? I say. You mean the Wee Willy Winkies. They come round every night. I'm standing upright and unable to move. The gunfire, the clap clap, clap he was shooting at me. That was just Grace protecting her own. She takes my hand. I ask her, who is Grace? Where you been? She asks. I say, There and back again to see how far it is. Nothing more is said.

She leads me across the road and gently knocks on the green door. It opens and she says, Meet Grace. I say in reply, Hello Grace; you look like Grandma Proctor but you are black and she is white. We walk in and the green door shuts to behind us.

Grace says, you're the man who is looking for the King and you know Henry too. He found me down by the Mississippi, I say, in some bushes and mud. He knows your King, Grace says. Yes, I say, I have seen the photograph. I put my hand into my pocket to check if it is still there. It is nice and safe. Yes, she says, it is his pride and joy. Dear Grace, how sweet you sound.

You see Elvis, Jill says, when I found you on Grace's land I didn't know whether you had arrived or you was just leaving. I don't know myself if I am honest. I just know that I am dying. You had this confused look about your face, she said, as though you didn't know whether you was coming or going...

I once was lost and now I'm found...

...whether you would be staying or leaving. And she makes an imaginary line, a dividing line and Grace asks so which side are you on son? It is as simple as that.

It was grace that taught my heart to fear and grace my fears relieved

Now think carefully before you speak, which King is it you are trying to seek? asks Grace. And before you start to sing, continues Jill, is it the illusion or the real thing? And when your search is at an end what is it you intend? To kill the King, but I don't know why, I reply. In this place, I say, your blackness holds no fear. Why is that do you think A phone rings.

Grace says, hello, turns to face me and with a smile that would warm a million hearts in one go, she says, it's for you. I ask, who is it speaking please? Hello son, it's your dad. Your mum is asking son when you will be *home*. The phone dies. I shout Dad! Please don't go, and the green door opens on the sun.

How precious did that grace appear the hour I first believed grace will lead me home?

Oh, you're back, the voice says. I open my eyes and I'm looking at the interior roof of a car. I turn my head and see the face of George Montgomery looking at me. You're back with us man. I got worried there. I say to him, are you arresting me? He laughs, man where have you been? You went to sleep on me man. I didn't know what to do. You said you needed to go back to the hotel to pick something up and on the way there you fell asleep. But I couldn't wake you so I left you to sleep.

How long have I been a sleep? Oh, about an hour. I can't remember getting into the car. You were down by the Mississippi sitting on a park bench looking content with the world. I asked you if you wanted to see where the King lived, you got in and after about, oh, I don't know, perhaps five minutes, you fell asleep. Sorry. Don't be man.

I hope you don't mind me asking, but how are you? I mean yesterday an' all. I say, I didn't expect it to be so hot. He says, it's August its allus hot in August. Oh by the way your friend Priscilla said to meet her. Where? She said in the little café at the bottom of Beale Street. Do you know where it is? Yes, I saw it earlier.

I'll take you. No it's okay. He starts up the engine and we move away.

We stop outside the café and I can see Priscilla sitting at a table near the window. I say to myself, I wonder how long she's been there. George says, She been there a good half hour. I give him a glance and ask him if he wants to join us. But he refuses with a shake of his head and murmurs something about having things to do. I get out of the car and say thanks and sorry again. He drives off.

Priscilla notices me and waves me in. I have sweat lining my back and my shirt is sticking to me. I walk in, find the table she is sitting at and sit down opposite her. She's kept her fifties tomboy look. She smiles and asks me if I would like a coffee. I say yes and something to eat. I'm starving. I've not eaten since last night. Eggs, would you like eggs? I'm goin' to have eggs. George said he found you down by the Mississippi. I mumble a yes and pick up the menu. You fell asleep in the car, he said. It seems that way, I reply without looking at her. I have nothing to say. It happened; I have no explanation. Like I said to George it must be the heat.

I look up and there is a tall black man walking towards the table. I drop my eyes to the menu and pretend to read. He says to Priscilla, Is this the man you've been patiently waiting for? I look up at him and he is staring at me. Haven't we met? He asks. With a nagging doubt in the back of my head I say I don't think so and go back to the menu.

So what are you good folks eating? Priscilla leans back in her chair looks up at him and, smiling, she says eggs, my good fella; we have decided to have eggs, sunny side up. Is it goin' to be one or two? I say two each and he walks away and disappears behind a plastic curtain.

Crudup is singing. Pictures of Ike Turner and Rufus Thomas are on the walls around the café. I say to Priscilla, I like this better. So do I, she says smiling. The tall black man arrives with the eggs and Rufus Thomas is walking the dog and the man says, do you know that dog spelt backwards is god? Priscilla replies, and do you know that god is dog backwards. Silence hangs heavy like we are all waiting for a time's up buzzer to go off. He stretches his arms to the ceiling and shouts Hallelujah, relaxes and says, makes you think, doesn't it? And then walks back behind the curtain.

Priscilla asks me what is the difference between sunny side up and eggs over easy? I say I know this one and tell her that eggs over easy are fried on both sides and sunny side up is fried only on one side. But these taste like they are fried on both sides. Don't you think so? I take another bite, look at her and say, I don't know. You would have to try both in order to make a judgement. She nods her head and between mouthfuls she says, who cares anyway. We eat the rest of the eggs in silence.

We finish the eggs at the same time, line our knife and fork up in the middle of our plates at the same time, and push the plates to the edge of the table at the same time. We sip some coffee at the same time, put our cups back onto the table at the same time and then she asks me my age. I look at her expressionless and say, why, does it matter? I take five dollars out of my pocket and put it under the ashtray in the middle of the table. I get up and leave the café without giving her an answer.

The sun is blazing hot. She stands next to me, hooks her arm in mine and says, Sorry. I'm thinking should I lie? Instead I say, I'm not ashamed if that's what you mean. No I don't mean that. I pull away and walk down Beale to Front Street. Priscilla catches up with me. People have said I look ten years younger than I really am. Front Street there is a Front Street near where I live.

It was on Front Street where I kissed for the first time. It was in the doorway of the Liberal Club. We got married six months later. She was pregnant. I loved her lots so it didn't matter. Soon after, the second Lorrie came along. I still loved her but the King started getting in the way and the miners were into the tenth week of their strike. He killed it for her. It's him or me she said, crying. I didn't cry. I am fifty-three.

We are on the grass verge and walking down towards the Mississippi. Tom Sawyer comes to mind and I say God this river is wide. We stop to let a tram go by. Tom Sawyer comes to mind again. Priscilla says it is at its widest near Bena, Minnesota, twenty miles wide down there, or is it up there? The length of it is at least two thousand miles.

I ask her where is St Petersburg? In Missouri, she says. It is where Tom Sawyer and Huck Finn lived. I like Huck Finn, she says, I like Huck Finn more than Tom. They were both nice boys but Huck had this twinkle in his eyes, you know, this rebellious streak that would send him off on all sorts of adventures. He didn't even care if he was sent to hell for helping Jim. Would you care? She asks. Care about what? I say. About going to hell for helping a black man? She walks off ahead of me.

I follow her further down the bank. She stops in some thicket and sits down. I'm standing over her and I ask her what she means. She says, don't worry about it Elvis. Huck wasn't bothered that's all. In them days they would have hung him up; strung them both up alongside each other like caught rabbits. Come on sit down. I sit down next to her.

I ask her, have you read *Call of the Wild*. You see everything through the eyes of a dog. Don't you mean god, she says. I say, No, I mean dog. I was twelve years old. I got the book given me as a school prize.

That's nice, she says. I sit down and we both have our legs up against our chests. I got lost in that book. I felt the dog's pain. I ask her, how did you get on with the nigger word? She squeezes my arm and says, it is just a word. Yes, I say just a word but powerful all the same like a bomb I would say. And I continue, there was never any fiction in our house just Marx, Elvis and

Engel. A day at the races, I say. She laughs and says what a great combination. I laugh too. She stops laughing but I can't. I'm stuck on this rollercoaster of laughter and it's not stopping. I cannot get off. The laughing is killing me.

I fall onto my back and Priscilla is looking down at me, smiling at me laughing my socks off. Through my tears I watch her head fall closer to mine. The sun becomes an eclipse. Shadows form and her sweet smell of youth stops the laughing. Her lips fall onto mine. It's not a peck like my mam or would give me to shut me up. Priscilla's soft, warm, melting lips stay forever. They taste of eggs, sunny side up. The morphine would leave a nasty taste in my mouth and make my breath smell, the doctor said.

I place my hands gently across the back of her head and press her face into mine. I shut my eyes tight. Total darkness descends. The sun disappears. She explores my tongue with hers. I am lost in the heat of the day. My bits down below do not respond accordingly; tears well up instead. She slowly pulls her head away and lets the sun back in. She smiles and wipes a stray tear from the corner of my right eye. I roll away hoping the grass we are lying on will swallow me up and spit me out in little pieces small enough to be eaten by the worms. She pulls me back.

I can smell her sweetness; me down here and her up there. I close my eyes and lie still. I feel the grass wrap itself around me. The sun disappears. Priscilla's lips, hot and soft, are working their way up the scars on my gammy leg. *Impotency* is a strange word, imp like

irrelevant small things? Or is it *im...pot* like *ink pot*. That's what you do isn't it, you dip your pen into the pot. It's only human nature, after all, to take Priscilla behind a wall and pull down her protection and slip in your connection; but still no joy.

The doctor apologised when he told me. It's not your fault, I said. Still, he said, it's a bore. No, I said, it's a bastard but, hey, I'm going to Memphis anyway. He laughed.

I'm looking up at a clear blue sky. I feel her soft gentle lips kissing my deceased flesh and I sing

Have you ever been lonely have you ever been blue have you ever met someone who doesn't like you?

Blackness swallows me up. A sharp excruciating pain surges through my right hip. I descend into hell.

I grab at the hip and scream, Bastard! And close my eyes again. I slowly open them. I am frightened to see. The pain is raging. A policeman holding a truncheon in his hands is looking down at me. The sweet smell of Priscilla has disappeared. Just a cold wind remains. George, I ask, is that you? I feel cold. His chilling stare digs in deep. The truncheon is above his head ready to fall. It's that nigger word isn't it, George? His laughter is bursting my ears. I shut my eyes tight again and wait. The doctor said that that is all I can do.

Have you ever been lonely have you ever been blue?

Every Sunday morning, Mam would sing the same song.

Have you ever met someone who didn't like you?

It's the only one she ever sang that wasn't the King's. Am I dead yet?

The question to ask, my man, is not whether the word is wrong but did Jim mind being called one? The silence does not respond. I sit up and the water's edge is littered with garbage. I stand up in overgrown grass being weighed down by a darkening sky. The night is lying heavy; the air is pulling in the stench from the river's edge. I am dead. This is hell.

Have you ever been lonely have you ever been free?

I close my eyes and the ground is pulling me in. I go deep deep down underground, first my feet and now my crown, my tainted crown.

Have you ever kissed someone that looks and feels like me?

The ground is waste, left barren by the bombs. Norm and me smell dock leaf, the sun radiates a perfect heat that spreads warmly across our bare back and arses whilst we frantically look around us to see if anyone can see us exploring each other, bringing each other to a glorious finish.

Norman says, tell me, Elvis, and feel free enough to say, as the cool Mississippi runs through my veins, tell me does that hurt? I open my eyes and Priscilla's face is blocking out the sun. Her hand is exploring my crotch. No, I say, I don't feel a thing cos it ain't got that swing doo wop e do wha wha. There is nothing because there won't ever be. Not now not never amen to that.

I reach down and with a sorry smile I remove her hand from the dead place. Is it the age gap? She asks. I say, No, it's just the bloody alien that is eating away my insides. I shout, I tell you what! She eases herself onto her knees, onto her feet and straightens up. The sun reappears in all its glory and blinds me momentarily. Not for long, unfortunately, because I catch her brushing the remnants of dead earth away from her clothes, reminding me with her every stroke of what might have been. She turns and walks away. I shout out as loud as my lungs will permit; Wots it knows whats what.

Time passes. The sun eases. The Mississippi still rolls on and my watch is telling me that my life is rolling on still. What to do hey? I ease myself up onto my elbows to see what this world has to offer. My watch tells me my song has been sung. The moment has passed. What to do hey? There goes my everything. So the song says. I look at my watch again.

People are milling: short, fat, pink, white, black, with a quiff, hair long, blonde, short, bobbed or black. They don't notice me sitting here on the long green grass on the banks of the old Mississippi, and that's the way I like it. I like it ah ah.

In a minute, the pain is going to kick in again. It's going to hurt because that's what pain does, it hurts. So I think I might just sit here, and then lie here, and then die here because I cannot think of a better place to be than on the bank of the old muddy Mississippi where once Henry Fuller found me, in another world, trying desperately to breathe.

But I won't because I'm scared to. I am scared of dying. There, I've said it loud and clear for all to hear. But who isn't? I know I have said I wasn't. But I was fooling myself and trying to fool you too. Them, I reckon now, that say they aren't bothered, are lying and anyway, how would you know you wasn't scared? Until you have reached that drop-off point, how would you know how you would feel? Take no notice. I'm just waffling. Anyways, if you find yourself standing and wobbling on the edge of a cliff you'd be scared then, that's for sure. Isn't that how it would be? Anyways, with the sun on my back, I'll just sit here and contemplate my navel. That's the way ah ah I like it.

I like that phrase, contemplate is a great word. I'll think about what might have been. But what is that supposed to mean, what might have been? When, what might have been, what if, what if. Okay, what if I hadn't been in the house in sixty-eight, would I be here now? But I would have been in the house in sixty-eight because I was just twelve years of age and it was New Year's Eve and I wanted to be with Norm.

It's a funny age is twelve. So the experts say. It's the age when we are open to anything the world wants to throw at us. It's at twelve when we kids are in desperate need of a role model, so the experts say.

If my dad had thrown a few smiles at me when I was twelve, or ruffled my hair in a playful manner, I might have said no to my mam when she said come on sit down next to me. But I didn't. I sat down next to her and let her ruffle my hair instead. I ruffled my lad's hair and smiled at him, but Lorrie took him anyway. It was all my fault. Oh, woe is me, isn't that how it goes? Give me the boy till he is fifty-three and I'll give you the man. Should I stay or should I go? Isn't that how it goes? The pain is telling me I should leave.

Main Street is busy, busy with people hanging, chewing the cud and giggling aimlessly. There are fat, thin, oblong men doing their best to gyrate all over the steps and what a mess they are making. There is Priscilla, my beautiful Priscilla, leaning casually against a white solid pillar with legs crossed and nose pointing north, enjoying a smoke of sorts and hanging with Henry who is standing in his green tweed suit behind an oversized overripe near to death Elvi and mimicking the poor man's version of Bridge Over Troubled Water. When has Henry felt down and out and small?

Priscilla is laughing uncontrollably and they don't see me so I walk on and wonder what the hell I am doing here. Morphine brings sweet relief from what might have been. It is nineteen sixty eight.

Grace is smiling at me. I raise my arm in response but it's pulled back down by Jill who is holding on to me tightly. What are you doing man? Waving back why? You can't do that you know you can't. She pulls at my arm and I follow her. Where are we going Jill? She replies, You'll see.

The marchers control the road. Hundreds are marching with banners held high. Women and young children marching with their men folk; *I Am A Man* they all scream in unison. We dodge the white folk, zig zagging in and out, like we have some place to be soon. These others they don't see not like us they don't. Busy they are booing and hissing and screaming, Get back to work, you lazy niggers. The police are with them, laughing and giggling like chatty school children enjoying the playground. It is all a big joke. Over the road is majestically standing Orpheum Theatre showing the film *It's A Mad Mad World*.

We reach them that are leading the way. See Elvis, see there. Where Jill? What am I looking at? Not what, Elvis, but whom? You mean Henry? I mean Henry and the man linked next to him. Trying to keep up is tiring and the crowds are making it difficult to see where she is pointing. The yelling and the screaming and the laughing is crowding me in. I can only just see Henry in his long dirty coat, the one I wore what seems like only a moment ago. Jill is whispering and I have trouble in listening and Jill is insisting, Look look it's the King.

Isn't it grand!! Isn't it fine!! Look at the cut, the style, the line.

I squeeze in between a policeman and, arms swinging, screaming, I am trying to get a closer look at the vision, jostling and pushing my way to the front, desperately trying to grab the scene by the throat and shake it all up.

It's the King the King the King!!

Applause and murderous expletives drown out the crying that is driving me forward to the edge of my oblivion.

The King is in the altogether the altogether.

Jill is tugging at me desperately, trying to hold back my tears. I have to Jill, I have to destroy, and I stare at a George Montgomery dressed in his brand new freshly-pressed uniform whispering to me, All in good time Elvis, all in good time.

A gun goes off and glass is smashed and flailing bodies hit the ground.

Bang!! Bang!! Pow!! You what you what you what!!! Poor Larry Payne is dead.

Women scream and men shout for calm. Jill and me hit the wall; I can't feel the ground under my feet. Through the mayhem I see Henry with a preacher man push a round face black man onto the back seat of a car. The car drives away at speed. People fall into the space the cars have left and run for their lives away from the smacking of heads and the smashing of more windows.

Which side are you on, boy? Which side are you on?

We are running to anywhere that is out of reach, down Main, past wooden windowed shops and people huddled together afraid in doorways. Some brave black face screams out: Its war, man, its fucking war! *Larry Payne is dead.*

We turn left on to Mulberry and slow down. I see the motel ahead of me. *I Am A Man* and I am fifty-three.

Above my bed, the air conditioning whirs and rattles and stops dead in its tracks. I lie drowning in gallons of sweat. The sheet beneath me is a funny looking grey and stinks of unclean bodies. I am somewhere else I have never been before I know I am in hell. I can tell. I lie still, unable to move, immobilised by fatigue. I know I am fifty-three and still a man, but the darkness baffles me. I prop myself up and try to make sense of it all. Pieces of newspaper scatter the floor. I pick one piece up and it says, April 3rd 1968. A rifle leans up against a wall next to a chair. A glimmer of light catches the corner of my left eye. I turn to face it and see a bath with a window above it and light coming through it.

Journey into Space

I drop from the bed onto all fours. The floor smells of piss and a big brown rat, as big as my hand, scuttles past. I grab the side of the bed, in fear of my life and ease myself up onto my feet. I stand stiff for a while to let the buzzing stop and walk to the light. I drag my gammy leg behind me. The floorboards creak the tune to my worst nightmare. The bath is made of tin and is badly corroded. A pan of steaming hot water sits on the bottom of it as if waiting. There is a musty smell and yellow wallpaper hangs loose next to the window. Dingy grey lace curtains hang from it. I have a fancy to pull the yellow wallpaper from the wall but a big orange spider rests behind the fold and stares through my eyes and into my soul. A neon sign flickers behind the lace on off on off on off on and off on and off

I have just found joy I am as happy as a baby boy playing with another choo choo toy since I met my sweet Lorraine.

I am fifty-three years of age and I am a man. If you say so, honey.

I open my eyes, I am lying on the bed again, and a black woman with plenty of bosom is sitting next to me. Mae Ray, I say. I turn away and the smell of Magnolia fills my nose and I feel the sun on my face and the ground beneath me is made of grass and a hand with gentle ease pulls me round and I say Grace. It is Priscilla's hand.

You fell asleep. I say, I thought you had gone. I watched you walk away. I saw you standing on the steps with Henry. You was both laughing at an ugly Elvi gyrating. Henry was standing behind him mimicking him. I'm not going to say anymore. That's okay Elvis, you don't have to. Then why are you still here? I ask her sharply. She takes my hand and says to me, because I am Priscilla and you are Elvis. The kiss comes crashing through the mist and I pull my hand away.

It doesn't matter, she says, and takes my hand back again. I don't resist, but feel awkward and silly. I say, what is the time? You know, I don't know, she replies. I make a chuckling sound through a closed mouth. Priscilla responds with the same sound. I look at my watch and it is four thirty. How long have I or we been here? Not long, she says. You've been asleep most of the time. I didn't want to wake you or leave you. You seem disturbed. Will you do something for me? I ask her. Of course I will.

You know Priscilla, we know nothing about each other yet within two days of meeting we are sitting in the long grass by the Mississippi holding hands – you a young woman and me an old man. She smiles at me in a way only she knows how and says, yes, it looks that way, doesn't it. Will you do me a favour? Will you come with me to the Lorraine? She squeezes my hand and says the sweet Lorraine of course I will. You have an urge, she says, and I think it is the right thing to do.

Her tone makes me feel tiny and I recoil back into my shell. She lets go of my hand and stands up with great energy, as if it is an emergency. I watch her brush away grass bits off the back of her legs and gently rippling bum and walk off in the direction of Main.

    I remain seated and wonder if I have made the right decision. Sleep still haunts me. She stops, looks back and beckons me to move. I ease myself up on to my shaky legs still not sure of anything except that I am a fifty-three-year-old man with no spunk who is hopelessly lost in his dream.

    The sun is cooler now and we are on Main Street walking north alone. This is a strange city, I say. It seems to be only you and me. She squeezes my hand. This is where it began, she says. You Adam and me Eve alone in a city that knows no time, reason or rhyme; it just marches on keeping time with its own tunes alone trapped in its own mad mad world.

    I'm dying, I tell her. And she replies, I know, Henry is dying too. The demons have him like they have you. I am here to ease your pain, she says. Who are you Priscilla? She replies. I am your carer your provider your lady in waiting. And she smiles. You tell me, she says. And I smile because now I understand. Walking down Mulberry we skip and we sing:

Here we go round the mulberry bush the mulberry bush the mulberry bush here we go round the mulberry bush on a cold and frosty morning.

Priscilla leaves me and goes to a woman who looks like Jill. She is standing on Protest Corner. They kiss and hug and hold each other tight long enough to morph into one another.

A young Henry, the Henry from my waking dream, is standing under a balcony. Look, Henry. There's a reef of poppies hanging on a green door. Yes, he says. And we enter through the door below that says Going Down! To where it all began.

I am alone again, this time saying sorry to a frightened fresh faced Emett Till and watching in vain, too frightened to move, the young black lads and girls being beaten round the heads and hung from trees like strange fruit. Okay Dad, I cry, it didn't happen in our backyard but isn't it the same as you on the picket lines in eighty-four and these the same young black men and women refusing to move desperately trying to hold to their dream like you was yours?

And this Dad, isn't this the same type of bone-shaker bus we sat on once with Mam going on our holidays in them days of illusionary fun when you and me laughed and joked without reproach and Mam looked on with a frog in her throat, dying to laugh but daren't? Why was that Dad, why was that? He can't answer so I sit at the side of Rosa Parks. And the driver screams, Get to the back you can't sit there!

I want to shout back: Not on your nelly! But I'm too scared. And the driver shouts it again and again and Henry says to us both, from the back of the bus, leave it son, it is what it is, and Rosa agrees.

So I just sit and listen to the driver repeat over and over and over again the same few obnoxious words that would, unbeknown to him and Rosa Parks, change the world forever. Then the King would sing, in turn, the Hound Dog song.

I stare at three young men dressed in well-worn dirty clothes standing next to a dilapidated old refuse truck. It's you Henry, I say. Yes, me and Echol Cole and Robert Walker in 1968 on the day the King's daughter was born just before Memphis erupted and its people divided into their true colours. I tell him I have the picture. He smiles. So I went hammering on the boss's door and found no answers. The night is settling in through the stained glass window and Henry has gone like a puff of smoke. The Genie has left the room. I walk away too.

I found my thrill on Mulberry Hill. It lingers until my dreams came true.

It is black as tar on Mulberry Hill. I walk down in eerie silence. There are no elvi's down here on Mulberry Street. It's merely incidental in their scheme of things. Just somewhere to visit when caught in the rain.

The wind in the willow plays a sweet melody.

The night has drawn in. I look at my watch and see that time is running away from me fast so I hurry on – clip clop clip clop – the best I can, leg permitting. Clip clop clip clop. A trolley bus is coming. I make a dash – clippity clop clippity clop. The nearer I get the heavier my legs become – clop clump clop clump. The stop has gone my breathing too, one two one two and down I go with a big fat bump.

You okay there mister? A young black face asks. You sick? I tell him I'll be okay and the tram goes on its merry way without me. Are you dying mister? My breathing settles long enough for me to say yes but not now not yet and I am able to stand erect one more time. I manage a smile and ask the boy his name. Larry

Payne mister, Larry Payne he says. You might have heard of me; I died in sixty-eight, and he winks at me. Elvis Presley, ain't it so? I say, Yes how did you know? Man, it wasn't hard just one look that's all it took, and he produces a high pitched laugh and shouts, I told you so, I goddam told you so, you incognito or something? And he winks. You trying to get to the end of the line, mister, aren't you, and you've just missed the bus? Well you stay there.

Larry leaves, goes down the street to where a rickshaw is parked. He gets onto the bike and rides it back to where I am leaning up against the wall of a café where faces with prying eyes are glued to the glass like they are watching the latest movie where a black lad kicks a white man's ass.

Larry what you got there? I ask. He gets off the rickety old bike and walks towards me. It's my dream machine Elvis my man, and like in them movies you was in it's going to get you to wherever you are wanting to be. Your wish is my command. Please I'm late for a very important date are you sure? You seem to be young for your age. I am the same age as you were when you were my age so it is up to you.

It is an ancient bike like the one my mam used to ride and we glide along oblivious to the world outside. Cars pass us and clouds gather and I sing:

It don't mean a thing if it ain't got that swing do wop he do do I.

Busy Beale boogies by to listen to Reverend Green praise the lord and give thanks to God for this week of hedonistic Elvi fun. A blues band plays a slow lament and Larry Payne starts singing:

I got shot the other day on the street of old Beale and now I have gone to heaven. I said I got shot the other day on the street of old Beale and now I have gone to heaven.

Do you know Henry Fuller? I ask. Yes mister, everybody in Memphis knows Henry. Henry is my friend. Do you know where he lives? I ask. Of course I do man, I told you he's my friend. Can you take me there? I ask. You want me to wait for you? Wait? Wait till after. Wait till after what? I ask. You got a song to sing ain't you? No, is my reply. So I will wait for you. No I want you to take me there now. But you gotta sing man. You knows it's important to you man. Ain't that what you here for? I don't know that Larry, the judge is still out on that one. Well you're the boss. I just drive a rickshaw for my sins.

What sins are they Larry Payne? Oh we all got sins man. Can't escape the old sins, that's a fact. Being in the wrong place at the wrong time seems to have been a sin to them that make the rules, only they didn't have to shoot. Who shot you Larry Payne? They all did brother. They all ripped through my body like a real old mean machine. One minute I'm in school the next I'm on Beale gasping for breath. They didn't need to do that. I wasn't already dying like you. I wanted to live.

But you can't argue with the man upstairs. It's what I tell Mae Ray when she complains about old Henry. I say, let it be Mae Ray he ain't like you and me. The old man upstairs, he made him different. Old Henry, he cares. Black and white it makes no difference cos that's how he sees it. Not like me. Black on white that was me. And I paid for it.

My body moves to the rhythm of his voice and to the sounds of Beale echoing through the cobbled street beneath us. Is it far? I ask. He lives on Hernando but you already know that. You have been there before I suspect. That's nice. I ask, is it a dark secluded place. A place where nobody knows your face a place my old man knew well

    I wouldn't know mister I just drive a rickshaw. Clip clop clip clop clip clop. *Treat me like a fool*, clop, *treat me mean and cruel*, clop, *but love me*, clop. *Take this faithful heart*, clop, *and tear it all apart*, clop, *but love me*. And sleep pulls me in or so it seems.

I wake staring at a grey lampshade that has a torn lace frill round its edge. Opposite where I lie is a window with green curtains each side. I hear children singing:

Georgy Proctor is no good chop him up for firewood when he's dead put him to bed poor old Georgy Proctor.

I swing my legs to the floor and hit my foot on a small brown dresser. It has a patterned white dish with a piss pot on it; my own bedroom. The room I got lost in with Buck the dog from the book Jack London wrote.

I leave the bed and walk to the window and pull back the green curtain. The sun is setting and my arms feel cold. Children are playing on the cobbled street below. They are giggling and laughing and throwing stones at my window. Who is that man? the freckle-faced boy with an iron leg shouts pointing up at me. He is wearing strange clothes and in my mam's room.

The door behind opens and a speck of light enters. My dad follows, young and fresh-faced. He is wearing across his chest in big bold black letters *I Am A Man*. Does he know what it means, I say to myself.

He is carrying a tray and on it is something hot. He walks to the bed and sits down. Gumbo son, he says.

Your mother made it. He puts it down on the chair next to the bed. Its spicy chicken and smoky sausage; too rich for me. He says, how are you feeling today? Has the pain gone away? Or are you still like me not knowing if it's real. I will never be like you, I say. Oh but you are son; a chip off the old block your grandma would say. You might try and fight it, deny it, but in the end. We were worried son, your mam and me. We thought you might have got in with the wrong crowd. You do know he's black?

    I ask him, what's with it across your chest? What does that mean? It is what it says son. It is what it is all about for you for me. Is Henry here? Yes son, he's in the other room with your mam. He is making her laugh with his silly anecdotes about him and your precious King. Did you know he was black? I did Dad, but now I don't; only I've got to give him his photograph back. You will see him soon enough son. Now straighten up because you have not got long to go. Is Priscilla with him? I need to know that too. Priscilla this, Priscilla that, no son, she is not. And why is that? Because she is not real and he sings:

Priscilla Proctor is no good chop her up for firewood when she's dead put her to bed poor old Priscilla Proctor.

See son, even the iron-leg fat kid with no name out there on the cobbled street knows it. But that is me out there, I scream, and I know nothing. He leaves the room. The speck of light disappears. The air conditioning unit is humming. I know nothing; I know nothing.

A toilet flushes and a door opens. Priscilla walks towards me gracefully, wiping her thin pale fingers on a white hand towel. Her skirt, grey with frayed pieces of lace hanging from its hem, swings nonchalantly from side to side across the middle of her well-tanned thighs. A green blouse thinly covers her soft round breasts and her new hair, like a big red moon, lights up the ever darkening sky outside. She is humming the same tune as the machine above my head. I say, a nursery rhyme I presume. Yes, she says:

A sailor went to sea sea sea to see what he could see see see.

And we all sing:

And all that he could see see see was the devil and the deep blue sea sea sea.

She walks to the chair at the end of the bed, sits down and crosses her legs. I say, what is that tune. I don't know, she says, it just popped into my head. There is a lot of thigh.

He said you collapsed. The poor man didn't know what to do. Luckily I was standing on the steps waiting for you. Where? The Civic Hall, she says.

I was sick. I get a whiff of vomit. She said, that's right, I've just finished clearing it up. You were there? I ask. She's looking puzzled. No, I mean here, look, and she points to a dark red spot on the floor near where I am lying. You collapsed on the tram and the poor driver didn't know what to do. He remembered you saying you wanted to get off at the Civic Hall so he stopped. He took you to the hall in the hope that there would be somebody there who knew you. I'm sorry, I say. You asked him if he knew Henry. We brought you back here, me and George Montgomery.

I told the man at reception that you were drunk. He helped me to bring you up here. Who Hank? No George. Why didn't Henry come back with me? I don't like the fat man. Why? He beats people up. He takes you to places you don't know and leaves you there. He seems okay to me. I don't know what I would have done if he wasn't there. He's always there. Good job to.

The driver said you asked him to take you to Hernando's Hideaway. But the gumbo? I say. You must have had it in the café. You picked up the tram outside the Arcade. Hernando's Hideaway a secret place where nobody knows your face, she says.

I fall back onto the pillow. The air conditioning has stopped singing and so has Priscilla. I don't think they will give you another chance. It's two times now you have missed. She gets onto the bed and lies down beside me. You sound like my mother, I say, and turn my back on her, lie on my side and tuck my knees into my chest. She has drawn the curtains. I ask her the time. I feel her lift her arm from the bed. I smell her perfume. It smells of danger. Nine thirty she says. I say, Nine thirty what? am or pm? I feel her move. I feel her hot breath on the back of my neck and she says pm.

The air conditioning is singing a different tune and I lie listening in silence and I say, His name was Larry Payne. He told me he got shot by people unknown in sixty-eight. The year the King and me reinvented ourselves.

Her left arm, soft round breast and knobbly knees mould themselves, without effort, into my thin grotesque flabby flesh. Her hot breath on my neck relaxes me. The other guy in the photograph, the big guy with dark glasses, Henry called him Robert Walker and the other smaller guy wearing a flat cap that was Echol Cole. The lonely moon, turns the curtains a crazy yellow and the air conditioning sings a soulful tune of regrets.

Priscilla's soft round breasts have gone. I'm on my back. I stretch my arms out from my sides like an angel does when it starts its flight. The large blood stain mark on the floor makes me feel sad. I have woken up into an unexpected new day. It seems a long time ago when I last said hello and good morning how are you to myself.

EP: I'm well thank you and you?

GP: Me well, I'm dying but don't let that put you off because it hasn't me. No not now I am in the land of my dreams and that my friend, is all that matters. The rest is lies, mere propaganda, but thanks for asking.

EP: Why are you here?

GP: Well I will tell you. I am, apparently, looking for the King. That's right; do you know where I can find him? Which one? You ask. Well that is a conundrum. Why? Well unknown to me, I want to kill him or perhaps both.

EP: Is that right mister? So are you mad?

Then they all disappear. Henry, Grace and Echol Cole with the flat cap and frowning face. Back in 1968 when the King reappeared in a different guise and poor old George Proctor died.

Georgie Porgie pudding and pie kissed the girls and then he died.

I am naked on the bed spreadeagled waiting for my destiny to come. I lift my arm to look at my watch but it has stopped dead in its tracks. I don't remember. It's what happens. It is part and parcel of the whole scenario thing. No point in worrying about it. It is no good thinking about it. It is here and it is now and there is no escaping it: this great big *it*. I woke up, I think, so we should leave it at that.

I swing my legs out of the bed and plant them firmly on to the ever increasing blood stain on the floor. My body pains me. My arms, legs and head hurt me. What day is it really and what does it matter? I stand, stretch the best I can, and pull the curtains open so the world outside can see my nakedness

Look at the King, he's in the altogether he's altogether as naked as the day he was born.

Can you see my scars and what is left of my dick, Memphis? I can see you, Lauderdale again and the white church. I wonder if Henry's down there praying. Memphis you have opened up into a bowl full of glorious colours: different browns and different greens different yellows and different blues crisscrossing your tall flat-roofed buildings that hide deep your own buried, unwanted fears.

The sun is out the sky is blue there is not a cloud to spoil the view but it is raining raining up my arse

And the day rolls into one big enormous fart.

What to do hey where to go? Ladies and gentlemen the winner is me:

Well isn't it rich isn't it oh!!! Look at the charm of every stitch!

Love her and take care of her! I scream, as I watch her ashes dance in the breeze over her own beloved city of dreams, remembering her face beaming at me from the sofa on that cold New Year's Eve and her warm breath on my neck pleading with me to believe, squeezing the life out of me. Promise me George, promise me. I promise Mam please I can't breathe. It is our little secret son yours and mine to keep hidden whilst he's out there in the cold night trying to change the world snuggling up to his comrades down in the deep dark abyss you've got to fight George, you got to fight for the right to be. And on went the songs

Return to Sender, In the Ghetto and Love Me, Love Me.

First you learn the words George, then you perfect the style the style his style:

Isn't it ohhh! Isn't it ahhh! Isn't it absolutely wheee!

You Were Always On My Mind, wonderful stuff.

Then he died. Oh how he died a glorious death lad, a glorious death, said Ken. His lungs got him in the end, don't you know; Emphysema lad, emphysema.

Tall and tanned young and lovely the girl from emphysema goes walking

Ken said, it didn't walk son, it eat through him like a thing possessed. When I asked Ken if he struggled alone he said, no, son, he had me. But you're black, I replied. And he said: If needs must lad, if needs must. The world outside had lost its appeal.

Bathroom, blood, shit and lots of it, shower and dress then out there to where the balance of life has changed to find the King. The little hotel restaurant, where it all began, is near empty but for a group off Elvi's in the corner and football on the wall above their heads.

Their chatter is like an automatic drill determined to the end to dig dig dig. One of them waves, big quiff in his hair and leather jacket to boot has stepped off the mystery train. I'll have to try and get down to the café they sat in. What was it called? Oh yes, the Arcade.

The quiff man shouts, Hello tee-shirt man, you were good. I say Thanks. How long has it been now? He asks. I shout and I smile: Two days two worlds, two lives. And I tell him: damn parasite is what they are. That is what we all are, parasites. Why? Because we are all responsible for producing the very thing that spends its time destroying the very thing it relies on to survive – us. It's crazy, just like life itself. Like *it*, my old man would say, we are responsible for our own destruction. It's the system we live in. My dad would say it's an organism that builds within itself its own mechanism of destruction. You see, he liked his Marx. And I told him, Just like families then. If you've got it don't waste it that is what my mam would say. And my dad would say, but it isn't his to waste. It doesn't belong to him; he didn't create it he stole it. Like the money from the gas meters and the chocolate bar. You should be with me on the picket line son, not wrapped up in somebody else's skin, wrapped up in somebody else's name, no son this struggle should be yours and mine. But I don't want to struggle no more Dad, I said to him. Not with you, with Mam, with the world with myself. Tonight, Jeremy, if that is what your name is, and the quiff man shrinks, I am going to kill the King. My dad, my honourable and misguided dad, don't look at me like that. Love me. Take my faithful heart and love me. You see, Jeremy, it is in here waiting, laughing in the wings, that's what it's doing the fucking thing is standing in the wings and laughing its fucking socks off leaving me here with my arse on the toilet and my head hovering over the bathroom sink. Hey, I've just thought, what a fitting way to die. It wouldn't bother me. But imagine the headline: Elvis Presley found dead in the bathroom for the second time.

The quiff man turns away from me looking petrified behind his quick nod of the head and his fake smile. I leave wondering where Priscilla is.

Another warm day grabs me by the balls – not much there to grab, I know – and takes me down Main and into the Civic Hall. Please sir, again. The nasty parasite got the better of me can I have another chance because I really do need to kill the King. It is what I am here for that is what I have come all the way from sunny Nottingham to do, I think.

I walk into the Arcade. Straight out of the fifties it has long red plastic seats, cream Formica tables and a hissing coffee machine. It is devoid of people except for George Montgomery, Henry and Priscilla sitting with mugs of coffee at the ready. How did they know? Priscilla watches me walk through the door. She waves me over. I don't want to go. I never thought I would say that to myself. What has changed? It is as if their presence has interfered with destiny like when some unexpected visitor knocks on your door. Do you answer it or just ignore it? I don't know but now I want to be somewhere else.

I walk towards her. She's wearing tight jeans and bobby socks and has pigtails in her hair – green this time. The fat man sits to their right still in his Hawaiian shirt and he is waving at me too. I hate this, I really do. Henry in his tweeds and Priscilla have their backs to

George. All three are staring at me smiling at me over eeny meeny miny mo. I stop in my tracks. I cannot choose. I don't want to choose. They are weighing me down. The hissing gets louder; the steam is filling the room. I smile back the best I can, point at my watch, turn and leave. What else can I do?

I turn left and scamper down Main till I come to a big brown building with lots of windows. I didn't want to be with Priscilla because she was with Henry. Perhaps that was it. Henry raises too many questions, too many surprises, too many frightening thoughts. Priscilla doesn't create anything but confusion. George brings death even closer and I am not ready yet, I don't think.

I enter the building by its side door walk among its glass frosted crumbling walls and wooden seats. In the distance a body stirs. It wakes up from another world. The sound of a noisy mystery train comes and goes. It and I are the only ones here. The silence weighs heavy. I'm intrigued so I walk on slowly not wanting to be seen. It is a man. Now I can tell.

The man gets up, stretches his arms towards the ceiling and turns his head towards me. I stop, but this time I don't want to run. I feel unafraid. He beckons me over. I hesitate but wave back. I am like a child who has been told not to talk to strangers. I stand rigid. Please George, I just want to talk.

I turn around to leave but he shouts, Please George, please stay. I know that voice. I just want to talk. I walk over to where he is sitting and look down at him. How did you know my name or is it a general term you use like Norm does with Bruce? He smiles and says, Norm your friend?

He is a scruffy white man wearing scruffy seventies clothes – a dingy red tank top and brown dirty flares. He has jet black tangled hair with a long grey beard. Are you God? I ask him and he laughs. Some people thought so once, he said. But it was too much to bear. Why do you ask?

It's quiet, I say. He nods his head in agreement. That is the way I like it George, he says in a deep drawn-out Southern drawl, no longer the hustle and bustle of days gone by. He knows my name. Sit down next to me, he says. You'd have thought this week would have seen it differently, I say. Tell me why. I sit down. What's going down this week that I should know about? It's the week they celebrate the death of the King, I say.

I am mesmerised by his deep blue eyes. How did you know my name? I am like your friend Norm. No you are nothing like Norm. Then why are you here? He asks, smiling. Why are you in Memphis, my home? To celebrate his death, I reply without conviction. But I'm not sure. Then go back to where you live, he says. Where is that? I ask because I don't know anymore and who are you anyway.

I can be your worst nightmare or your friend. The choice is yours. Do you know Henry? I ask. He nods his head and says I know Priscilla too; we were close many moons ago. But the way you're dressed, I say it's like you are stuck in time. It makes a refreshing change, he says. And those eyes are they real? I ask out of the blue.

He laughs and drops his head into his hands and raises it. Sure they are real, look. I jump back in the seat, fall to the floor and scramble quickly on to my feet. The two blue eyes are staring up at me from the palm of his hands. There are two black holes where his eyes should be. I shout GOD!

He laughs even louder while he drops his head into his hands again saying, not me son not me but some did think it once and they bought death to my door. Then he looks up at me once more and smiles with his eyes intact. No sir, it ain't going to help you one bit to know the truth of it. So go home mister where the real pain is.

You are the devil in disguise; I knew it. I feel sick. Go home son. And he sings: *Treat me like a fool, treat me mean and cruel but love me* just like the King. Are you the King? I scream. He smiles and sings: *Take my faithful heart and tear it all apart but love me*. And I hit him over and over again screaming, it's not my fault it's not my fault! And he screams back thank you for that as his crumbling body hits the floor. I wake up with my head over my bed in the room with four white walls.

My arm is being squeezed and I hear my name being said. Priscilla is staring down at me and smiling like only she can. Elvis, Priscilla, her smile brings me back into the world. I've just seen the King with no eyes. Now you see them now you don't. They were a radiant blue and he held them in the palm of his hand. I thought it was God but he turned out to be the devil instead so I hit him over and over again. But he didn't die he just smiled and sang. She says, whilst clearing up the vomit and blood from the floor, It was just a bad dream.

Bollocks, I say under my breath and lie on my back and look at the ceiling patterns which are forming faces appearing and morphing to make one big black blob, and the air conditioning is purring like a contented cat. She's wearing pigtails in her green hair and pink bobby socks decorate her slim ankles and she walks away. It was just a bad dream, she says over her shoulder and into the bathroom she goes. I can hear the tap running and she comes back with a glass full of water.

I sit up, my head is woozy and I take the glass from her sweet childish hand and drink it all in one go.

A Mae Ray special, she says as I hand it back and she takes it to the table. Mae Ray, I say under my breath and watch her drag the chair from under the desk and sit on it facing me with her legs crossed and her hands tucked into her groin and her back as stiff as a cable. I lie back on the bed and wait for what I know is coming; the third degree. She will go on and on and I will apologise and that will be the end of it because that is all they would be waiting for, an apology. I am sorry, I didn't mean to do it. I didn't mean to look up her skirt. I was on the floor and she opened her legs what else was I supposed to do I was eight and feeling lonely.

Elvis, what are you going on about, Priscilla asks. Up there, I say and I point my finger at a small hairline crack I hadn't noticed before. What and where? She asks and she lies down beside me to see. There. Yes, she says in a throwaway manner. Perhaps I should tell Hank. She leaves the bed and resumes her position on the chair. Why would you want to do that? Because the ceiling might open up all over me in my sleep and things creep into my brain. Are you real? I doubt it, she says. There is silence but for the gentle purring of the air conditioning cat. What time does the singing commence? An hour from now, she says. An hour you say. I scream out loud.

Come on now George. Your dad is waiting. He gets angry if you keep him hanging. There were tears in my eyes after she had said it. Why are you crying, Mam? Because I love you George, she screamed. Do you Mam, do you really? Do you really know what love is Elvis? Says Priscilla, smiling.

I raise my body on my elbows. Priscilla, why are you here? My elbows hurt and I manoeuvre myself up. Priscilla leaves her chair presuming to help but I wave her away like an irritant. The curtains are drawn. Why, I ask her, have you closed out the day? She says, because it was dark when I put you to sleep. And when was that? I ask, frowning some. Last night. Last night? I say. Not this morning. You have not been anywhere this morning, she says. I reply with a conclusive, Oh yes I have, but you wouldn't believe me if I told you. And I get up and see that I am naked as the day I was born. You should let me look after you George.

I shakily make my way to the bathroom and turn on the shower and step in. I'm not a shower person usually. Nor am I one of them people who stay for ever letting the water cascade over them. No, in out shake it all about that's me. Standing by the bath drying myself down, I get a glimpse of myself in the long mirror. I have lost weight since I've been here. It's not surprising. The doctor said. My ribs are squeezing themselves out through the wrinkly flabby flesh. I once had a proud bulging gut but not anymore, flat as a pancake now. I should be proud. But I do have a bright red face – from the tablets or just being here, who knows? Now I look like an unlit matchstick. My flesh feels tender and sore to the touch my dick looks like a shrivelled sausage. I rub it gently with the towel and think of Priscilla my chameleon, hoping that it will jump to attention; no such luck. I drop the towel to the floor, close my eyes and wrap my fleshy hand round it and it gets lost so I try and imagine us locked together, I rub harder and drag into the past, Jill, Norm, Lorrie and Mam. I let go quickly, Not Mam! I scream and freeze and drop my head into the towel and sob wildly. I see the dirty man with no eyes. Let me show you George. Let me in. George, are you okay? She must have heard me. It's okay. You know you should never lock the door. You don't know what might happen. Sorry nurse, it won't happen again. I get dressed and open the door. Priscilla is standing there.

I push past her, vigorously rubbing my hair with the towel. Sit down, she says, I'll do your hair. No, I say. I need to get ready for the day. Who are you anyway? I can't look her in the eye. I sit down on the edge of the bed and hold my head in my hands. I am conscious of my toupee moving. She says it doesn't matter. Of course it matters. Of course it does. It matters like hell. Who are you to tell me that?

Before today when I forget, I was at home packing ready to leave knowing the consequences of my actions because it has been my dream to be in Memphis. It is what my dream has been all about something I have already mentioned, I think. So I told myself if I win so be it if I die that too. They were the only things to think about. Everything was straightforward. I knew what I was doing. I was armed for the fight. I was ready for the battle. Then you happened. Henry happened, even the fat man happened. Crazy crazy days happened. Now I don't know. Now I'm lost. I hear her say, being lost is a good thing. We are silent I try and work out what she means. I look at her face long and hard. I try to take it apart bit by bit, eyes, nose mouth and ears. Peel off the skin and leave nothing. Leave nothing to look at and then perhaps she will disappear and leave me in peace to contemplate my own pain. Not hers. The four white walls surrounding me move closer to where I am laying.

Are you real? I ask her again. I mean you just appeared from where? I mean, I turned around and you were there. You are always there. Like some— she cuts me short, like some guardian angel, she says as she runs the comb gently through my flimsy hair. I whisper, if you want. She continues, you are not the only one, you know, there are millions more like you. I feel hurt by her remark. I look at her hard again, long and hard and I put her face back together again and I punch it, metaphorically speaking. What do you mean not the only one? I want to say, what do you mean, like a ghost like an apparition now you see it now you don't. And I play some silly game instead. I close my eyes and open them again behind my hands. Now you see me now you don't.

She says, close your eyes proper. Why? I ask. She smiles and I close my eyes and look at her imprint on my retina until it fades and then I open them and, surprise surprise, she has gone. It was an obvious conclusion to the event.

I'm a dickhead of the highest order. I tell myself she must have moved pretty quickly and fall asleep.

I suddenly realise that there is no television in the room and that is unusual; a room without a television is like a room without a view. I make up my mind; I am going down to sort this out because at this precise moment in time I want something to stare at, something that will turn me on and off without fear or trepidation. What sort of hotel is it that has no television in its rooms?

I get into another tee-shirt, a green one this time, and a pair of blue denim trousers. They feel loose. I march down to the reception area to ask why.

Excuse me, Hank. Yes sir, sorry sir, I will deal with your enquiry as soon as I have dealt with this gentleman. All I want to ask you Hank, is why is there not a television in my room? That's all. There is not a television in my room. I want to watch *Gunsmoke* and I can't. My old man he loved Matt Dillon he thought the sun shined out his arse. Why is that do you think?

The other man in his bespoke glasses and yellow shirt looks at me puzzled and tells Hank that it is okay, it's not important and he will catch him later. He sounds German. Hank and I watch him walk away and enter the lift and gracefully and without bother drift upwards to heaven. We turn and face each other and Hank smiles and I say don't you have beautiful white teeth.

I ask him, Are they real? Yes sir, they are real, is his stern reply. Yes, but you have had them seen to, right? I mean, nobody's teeth can be that real. I mean, naturally that real that white that pearly white and even. I can assure you sir, that they are real. And he pulls at them with his left hand.

They don't move. But I'm still not satisfied. Right, I say, right, and look at him hard and long and say, but the proof of the pudding is in the pulling so can I give them a tug? Then I'll know for definite and without question that you are not cheating. He takes the clean handkerchief out of his top pocket and hands it to me and I pull and I pull and I pull. I hand him back the handkerchief and he wipes his hand with it before putting it into his right trouser pocket.

Okay sir, you were saying something about a television not being in your room? Was I? Are you sure? Yes sir, I'm sure. Yes I was, wasn't I? Well, you know what, seeing your teeth as white and straight as they really are has sort of made the issue of a television unimportant. I hated Matt Dillon. Thank you anyway but I have to go. I have to be somewhere else.

I turn and leave with Hank's eyes drilling holes into my back and it feels great; out the door, turn left and on to fame and glory. My public is waiting.

Elvi's are swarming all over the steps of the centre chit chatting to each other as I enter the auditorium. They, like clockwork soldiers and together, stop their chit chatting and stare. I nod my approval at them saying Here I am the waiting is over so let's get on with the show.

The place is a hive of activity. I take it all in and walk down to the stage where a young man wearing a plain faded blue shirt is just finishing singing: *Wise men say only fools rush in but I can't help falling in love with you.* He is fourteen years of age. His dad has decided to stay home. The lad's mother rushes on to the platform and squeezes the life out of him. I remember it well. Gene Kruper, the well-known jazz drummer, asked sarcastically a long time ago: What does a young kid know about love? But he was wrong. You know love at fourteen as much as you do at fifty, trust me, I know.

The young man was good and the woman who is standing next to me whispering sweet nothings in my ear asks me if I'm better. Yes thanks. I'm back on track as they say. Good, she says, same song is it? Yes of course, is my reply, it's the only one I know. It is the only one I understand. There is no more in the repertoire.

So I stand and sing my song and the place goes wild. All the people won't stop cheering and I shout, Do you want some more? and together they all shout again and again:

Look at the King! Look at the King! Look at the King! The King! The King!

Elvis can sing there is no doubt about it. I jump off the stage with the applause tearing down the walls and the place collapsing, keeping the wailing and the screaming where it belongs. I walk down Main and onto the bone-shaking bus.

Rosa Parks is still sat, relaxed, tall and proud, in a long sensible coat and concertina hat perched gently on top of her long crinkly hair. The driver is still telling her to get to the back. So I shout back at him: You prat, she isn't going anywhere; I am! I go to the back and lie down and go to sleep.

I sleep it seems for ever. I wake and Rosa is still refusing to move. Good on you Rosa. It is easy for me to say it now, not then; no, then I would have crawled back into my hole like the rest of the world and pretended nothing happened whether I agreed or not, because that is what you do if you're scared of the consequences of your own actions. The courage is not just yours Rosa, brave as you are, but belongs also to them brave souls who support you and I ain't one of them. It's more right if you are white on the bus back in the fifties.

What could you have done that wouldn't have put you in danger, but meant you would have carried the guilt around with you like a massive tumour? My old man would have shrugged off the question by saying, its war son, so get used to it because it never ends and that is it.

Inside and outside it never does. I am in a battle I cannot win, that is conclusive. I am like the man staring at a swinging noose; all I can do is stand and stare:

What is life if full of care we have no time to stand and stare...

Norman my dearest friend, do you remember when we stood in that ring on opposite sides as friends tried to knock the shit out of each other with you knocking more shit out of me because I couldn't see the point of it all? Later, when our friendship became cement holding us together, you tried to ease my pain whilst this silent, not to be spoken personal enemy of mine, is knocking three bells out of me. Now you look on from the wings, hopelessly and comfortably (saying thank God it's not me), cheering and praying under your breath, lost in the knowledge that nothing is real. And that is how I imagine it to be how I want it to be but we both know it's not so.

But that is all I have left mate; the truth in the knowledge that I now couldn't care less. I sit with dear Rosa resigned to the fact that I have lost and the singing has stopped. Wow! Who'd ever thought you would hear me say that? And here's something else I can say with ease, I hate my dad with conviction and now I can hate my mother too and nobody can say any different.

Hey Rosa, what do you think of that? I bet you would have been horrified gel, if you knew that your son hated you and perhaps my mam would too, who knows? I'm sorry Rosa, for everything; for saying such things to a lady like you. But there is no one else here other than the bus driver up front and he is a man just doing his job. I bet that's what he said on the day you were arrested.

You see Rosa, I know about you. I got to know about you the first time I come here. I know about Montgomery and I know about Henry's friends in sixty-eight – Echol and Robert and Mae Ray. Priscilla she's been taking me to places in my head that I thought was long gone and still is. I ain't figured that one out yet. I think I'm still on the move and in my back pocket Mrs Rosa Parks, I have Henry and the King. What do you think about that then? Would you be amused?

I want to ask Henry about it but I never get the chance because I don't think he likes me but he's there in my waking dreams; but as my enemy or my friend? Winifred, Amelia, Grace and Jill too what about them? And let us not forget old George Montgomery in and out of his sanitised blue serge uniform ready to crack heads on the picket line in sixty-eight when all I wanted to do was sing.

Let no man pull you so low as to hate him....Dr King

Notice the young lad with the limp standing on the steps Rosa, alone. That's me. How long have you been there son? I say to him. I don't know mister, He says back. I'm waiting for my mam. My dad's not coming. I want to sing. How old are you son? Twelve sir, he says. I'm not mad you know just ill, I say and he smiles and says, I know I've heard you sing. No mad man could sing like you sing. My mam says the same. We are going to Skegness. My dad doesn't like me so he is staying at home. He said I am a waste of space. You are not son, I say, and don't take what he says to your grave because before long and, time travels so fast, there will be no space for you to be in and that is the tragedy that lasts until somebody says otherwise and it will not be me I can assure you of that.

He turns and limps away and catches up with his destiny. It is a woman in a purple dress who smiles and waves at me and I cry and cry and cry and hold on to Rosa for dear life. A hand on my shoulder turns me round and Henry is smiling down at me tells me it is time to go. I say, The King, and he says, Yes Elvis I knew them both.

The sunshine hurts my eyes and I can't see. I don't say anything. I just hold on to the guiding hand and we turn left instead of right, that much I do know and I still don't say anything.

Crump Boulevard, he says. Crump was the man, in the early bad days, who owned the lot. I mean from Beale and all of Main. It is a busy road we are on. I can tell that. He was the governor back when we had nothing. But he gave us the vote and it cost him everything. My eyes are opened by a run-down leafy street. This is my *home*, he says, and you are my guest so don't you take no notice of the ugly looks that are coming your way you are safe in my hands. I say, I've seen it before, Henry. That's possible, he says, did you know it's my birthday today?

We are standing in front of the house with two windows and a green door that is peeling like a sunburnt body and a wire fence surrounds it all. Above the door it reads: *THE HALL OF TRUTH.* We enter the house, he tells me to sit down.

It is a kitchen, smart and decorated in green. There is a clock on the wall it says quarter to four. Don't take no notice of that, Henry says it stopped ages ago. Why green? I ask. I like green that's all. I hate it, I say but I don't know why. This is where I have lived for near fifty years. Like me, I say. It's a long time in one place don't you think. It's my home, he says with a smile on his face. Do you want something to drink? I say okay but I'm not sure I'm not sure because now I'm beginning to worry about the decision I've made. Should I go through with it or leave it alone?

Are you on your own Henry, I ask. I have Mae Ray, he says do you take sugar? No thanks, I say. You got family? He asks. No they are both dead, I say. He has a shaky hand which causes him to spill. Sorry about that. That's okay. I'm dying, he says. Sorry to hear that, I reply as we watch the tea hit the floor. A bit of a drag I bet.

He sits down in the chair opposite me, leans back and lets out a sigh of relief. Nothing is said for what seems like ages. Is Mae Ray here? Yes sir, in the room on the chair next to my bed. This is going to seem strange Henry, but I've been here before. Yes I know. A beautiful young mulatto brought you out from the woods.

I knew him in Shake Rag, your King. A place just over the tracks where the poor stayed clumped together, black and white and made grey. We shared common ground you might say. We were just two young kids getting it together and laughing about. Then his ma and pa did a moonlight flit and landed up in Memphis. We saw each other at the gospel church and just nodded without saying a word. It wasn't Shake Rag. In Memphis black and white comes into it. Not grey, all white. Then I saw him again in the induction line. That time we didn't nod just stared in a different direction. In sixty-eight Lisa Maria, his beautiful girl, was born and Echol and Robert, on that same day, died in the back of a big old truck.

What is happening Henry? A lot my friend, are you scared? Where am I going? It's the waiting, I know, he says. I didn't think I would be when the moment came but now it's, well, too late to wait and see, is my reply.

He looks at me and smiles and says, there are still things to do so I can't say right now but you will know soon. Soon? Soon enough, my friend, he said, trust me man. I don't understand, I say with a cry in my voice. There are lots I don't understand George and we never will.

Henry, are you God? Because it's you I fear the most. You are the hidden agenda, the ghost in the machine. Call it anything you like man, he says. Okay I reply; you are the colour of my shadow, the colour of the dark I hated as a kid. You are the colour of death I feared coming up the stairs; the shadow with the knife that wasn't there. Now you just smile at me and you are making it worse. That is me done. But what do you want me to say or do brother, cos it is out of my hands what you think and feel, what's gone man, what's past. My dreams you mean? And your waking hours, he says.

Are you then a dream-maker Henry, or an illusion, a spectre, a paragon, a heartbreaker or just a fool-maker, is that what you are saying? Not me brother, you do that yourself you're in control; you have been since you were twelve but you just don't know it yet but you will.

All I have ever wanted to do since I was twelve was to be here. With me, he says are you sure it's not me you are looking for. No, I love the King. You don't love him son. You can't say that Henry and don't call me son, you don't know. I know George. Can I call you George? No, my name is Elvis Presley. No George, honestly. Honestly that don't mean shit the people in my head they don't mean shit. They mean everything to you George, because they are yours. They belong to you. You put us there because you wanted to. We are your creation. What like God's Adam and Eve? I don't believe in God, I say. Yes you do son. Everybody believes in God one way or another. Some just don't want to call it that. I scream for the whole world inside my head to hear, my name is Elvis Presley it has been since I was born. And when was that…George, he whispered inside my ear, you are here to kill: to do then die. You said it yourself. Let it go George. Let the battle commence. You are nearing the end. You want completion. You want to die.

I tell him, I didn't expect you to put your hand on my shoulder all gentle like. Now I want to cry. I feel my tears welling up. I am desperately trying to hold them back. Don't George, your mam would say. You will block up your tear ducts and get an infection and you don't want that, nobody wants an infectious disease. I'm looking down at the floor. No sir not that. I know blame the blacks and I'll throw in the gays for good measure too, he says and it don't matter none it don't matter because I ain't after you liking me son. I ain't your son… Dad and I grab him round the throat just like before and he screams: *It's me George, it's me you are looking for.*

You unlock this door with the key of imagination. Beyond it is another dimension....Rod Sirling.

I feel nothing at all. I shoot up off the chair and make my way to the door. I want to leave. I try the door and it's locked and I panic. Can I leave please? Nobody is keeping you here. You were in need of a drink so I gave you a drink. You were in need of me and here I am. I tug at the door handle and the door will not open. You want answers to what is going on in your head? Only you got them mister, only you got them.

I feel my heart pounding ten to the bar:

Pardon me, boy I bang at the green door, *Is this the way to my salvation?*

With a cold clammy right hand I tug on the door handle. Doors open when you figure out the combination, when you see, for real, what Memphis is all about. It ain't ten feet off the ground like it was said in the song. No sir, Memphis is made up of spilt blood, its singers and its songs of toil and wonder. *I Am A Man* and don't you forget it.

You are going to die mister, you knows that. We all knows that. The world knows that. So you see it's important that you know it too. I mean really know. Really know the consequences of your own actions. It's what will open the green door for you. My head explodes into a million pieces as it hits the floor; you what, you what, you what you what you what.

The runaway train went over the hill and it blew. The runaway train went over the hill and it blew. The runaway train went over the hill the last I heard it was going still and it blew blew blew blew blew.

Henry, my mam shouts, fancy getting an engine that won't go. I didn't know Lorrie I didn't know. It will be okay though cos there are only two days to go. Two days to you Henry, might not mean much. But to poor George that is a lifetime. We'll sort it Lorrie, just open the door.

Green door what's the secret you're keeping.

And from behind the door I hear dustbins rattling, a lorry revving, moving then slowing, men and women singing *One more river to cross* and then my eyes open reflecting my own room back home, and on the King falling from the wall. And behind the door Henry thanks the people for coming and sings their song;

happy birthday to you to George and happy birthday to me.

Uncle Henry is here to see you George, my mam shouts below stairs. No thanks Uncle Henry and I try and raise myself up on to my elbows but I can't. Say, thank you for the train George, she shouts. I shout back, but it doesn't fucking work. I fall asleep.

Tell me Uncle Henry, you are a man of the world, my mam says, so tell me what is the combination that will open the green door? It's the right numbers being joined together in the right way, he shouts. Like the track beneath the train, I shout back. That is right so until you know that Elvis, the train and life remain upside down; a struggle for most I would say wouldn't you.

Women are laughing and whispering behind the door. A beautiful melodic voice says not to be silly you can't go out in this not at your age so blow out your candle and eat your pancake.

Can I have some pancakes Amelia, please? Sunny side up or the other way round, I forget. Sunny side up, it sounds better. Everything should be sunny side up don't you think. Life should be sunny side up…

Get yours sunny side up up get yours sunny side up.

…before it's too late. But first you have to know what the numbers are. That is right man, you've got it.

I open my eyes and I'm back again. The bright sun makes the room feel warm. A lady is smiling; a black lady is sitting on the chair smiling with legs crossed. Always with legs crossed. Hello. Hello back, she says. You sleep a deep sleep, young man. The sleep of Kings, I say. Are you Mae Ray? I ask. Yes, that's me. Henry's not here. I think he's behind that door eating cake. Yes, I know. I'll wait. We allus say Hello in the morning, Henry and me. You Elvis I take? Yes, Henry said to expect you. He did? That's right.

He said you was white but I suppose with a name like you got you couldn't be anything else. I suppose not. Do you live here with Henry? I ask. In a manner of speaking I do, although I was late today. Late, how late can you be when the clock has stopped, I say. I'm usually here when he wakes. I bring in the day with him. I rise and shine him you might say. But you're here so I'll rise and shine you instead. What do you say to that Elvis? What do say to a little rising and a shining from Mae Ray? And I watch her leave the chair and make her way to the end of the bed doing a few dance steps on the way. Her mouth opens and out comes:

There's an old piano and it's playing hot behind the green door. Don't know what they are doing but they laugh a lot behind the green door.

I join in with the last line it seems to be mandatory so I don't have a choice. So stick you, Henry. She come and laid her body on me. She let me in. I am swimming in birth fluid. Then she is gone. Mae Ray, in the flick of an eye, has left the building.

I am the only being in the abyss of darkness. From the abyss of darkness comes forth my birth from the silence of a primal sleep.

I am sitting upright in a pool of sweat feeling fulfilled. I stand and bend and touch my toes one, two, three and four. My back really aches and my joints squeak. But I don't give a flying fuck. I leave the bed like I done before and walk to the chair Mae Ray was sitting on, get my clothes and dress. They smell sweet of Magnolia like they did before. I will leave it at that. I will not give it much thought. What I need to do now is leave.

I open the door onto another room. In the middle, on a table, sits a pancake with a candle in it and a nearly-finished piece of birthday cake. In the corner a model train is turned on its head. It stands erect like a soldier going to war. How does it do that? Just another door to get through then I'm gone.

I walk down a road invested with fruitless poplar trees. It feels far removed from Downtown, the centre with its sinister connotations. Is this the start? The road is long, wide and empty but for the odd one or two black men, dressed in old working denim, hanging around doing nothing but staring at me with their bulging eyes. The road seems to have no end to it; no reason or rhyme. The air is hot and clammy. I'm starting to wonder, is it the road to hell? It offers no crossroads. No overhead lights. Like Downtown. Is this suburbia with its big houses and its long drives? Not like Henry's house tucked away behind tall old trees a lonely mile or so away it seems now.

Egyptians called it a place of good abode; the magical city. And there it is a sign for Highway 51 – a way out of this insanity and off this aimless route march to home; Graceland this way. This way brother, this way son, this way fellows, let's have another one.

The roar of passing traffic and the hoots of car horns offer me the safety of a busy road and there it is, Calvary, on a hill not too far away: the King's domain majestically placed. My pace quickens and then slows. I feel like a weary foot soldier returning home from an unforgiving war; an unceasing battle with shadows that will not leave me alone. My pace quickens again. Give me the jungle room and then let me sleep. Give me a gal I can call my own. Give me a life that will never stop. Give me a home with an ever strong tick tock tick tock clock. A voice cuts me short.

Sorry sir, you can't walk up there. You can walk down but never up. It's the eighth wonder of the world, see. Going up alone is too much of a threat. You have to get on the coach with the others and pay the price like the rest, the voice, dressed as a cop, says. But it is such a lovely day and two hours is all I got, I reply with a smile that I hope will rot his gut.

No sir, you can take as long as you want as long as you have left before the doors are shut. Oh, the doors, them doors, them pesky green doors. No sir, they are white with big stained windows. Like a King's palace should be, you mean. Did you know that green was my dad's favourite colour? Is two hours all I need? Maybe so sir, I can't rightly say, maybe not, your decision, so they say. That's a shame such a lovely day. Certainly is sir, such a lovely day.

I come from over that way, pointing to the back of the King's place. Grace's land they say. A lovely lady is Grace. I can't rightly say sir. Do you know Henry? Everybody I have met says they do but I don't know you, so perhaps you don't. Perhaps you have to know me before you can know him or is it the other way round. His crinkly grey face gets angry.

Sir, I am going to have to ask you to leave. Go get on the coach or walk away. Walk away? No, I can't, not yet. Is the King home? I reach into my trouser pocket to take out the photograph of Henry and the King and a hand grips tight round my wrist. You hold on there Elvis my friend, the other voice says. Its George Montgomery dressed in an orange tee-shirt and he's glaring at me little old near dead me.

Hey George, how you doing, how's your belly for spots? I say, unmoved by the gun the other one has pointing at my chest. I say to him, Go ahead shoot. Can't think of a better place to be than this, and the copper laughs and says, Elvis why didn't you say? You old bafoon and puts the gun away. George Montgomery gives off a raucous laugh and pats me hard on the back and says, Elvis, meet Peter Muldoon.

Hello Peter Muldoon, how do you do? How's your belly for spots? Peter Muldoon says, Well I'll be, you should of said. Well how could I have said? If I had, you would have called a cop and called me crazy and laughed till your sides split. Just like the rest do.

Crazy? he says with his wizened face. Yes, you know, screw loose. Screw loose? he says not knowing what the hell I mean. Yes, you know, and I jab my finger into the side of my head and cross my eyes and stick my tongue out the corner of my mouth and sing the best I can: *screw loose, screw loose, put on your dancing shoes.*

Oh shucks man I was thinking you crazy anyways but if you had said your name then I would have shuck you by the hand and said welcome, welcome to Graceland. And he shakes my hand. Ain't that right Peter? I turn and face Peter looking for a response and he is smiling and nodding his head. He puts his arm around my shoulder and pulls me to him engulfing me in his stink. Okay Peter, okay if we go in? Sure George, go ahead but you going to be okay walking up that drive? You know what happened last time. Don't you worry about me, George says, smiling his toothless grin. I'm invincible. Then out of the blue Peter turns to me and whispers is it heaven or is it hell?

We walk with the sun burning the back of our heads. I ask him what happened last time. Oh that? I died. He doesn't say anything else. We walk on and stop next to a beautiful green weeping Poplar tree. He points at an undisturbed small raised mound of soil in the shade of the tree. Right there it was. I slid down that tree and died on my butt. I was just sitting there for the world to see. Ninety-three it was. It won't happen again and he walks on.

There it is, four white pillars standing tall behind two proud white stone lions sitting each side of some shiny steps leading up to the front door. I stand and stare in awe. A coach passes by and stops and drops people off. I stand and look at George choking, wondering why he is not again dead. You can't die twice, he says, if at all.

The people pop out of nowhere and take over chitter chattering and laughing in falsetto. They spread their arses everywhere sucking up the dead earth opening their other eye to see and collect memories to store in their dark forbidden places for the likes of you and me. I will call them parasites and yell at them to join the queue but they will not listen to me, just like my own chittering and chattering and laughing uncontrollably thing inside of me.

I have sung my song. Here take these and if the pain comes on take one but not now hey George? Are you listening?

Down the lane snow is glistening. It's a wonderful sight and we are happy tonight standing in this wonderland.

What do you mean I can't die twice? Will it be under a blossom tree George, you and me together holding hands over my dead body? The King he had his heart attack on the bog up there – the second room along, so they say. Bog it rhymes with dog, God and wog. Are all white people racist or just dead scared of their own shadow like me?

My dad waves me over and I go and sit down next to him on the steps and cross my arms just like he is doing. Isn't this nice he says, and I start crying. My mam, his wife, has died. He puts his arm round my shoulder I suppose to comfort me but it doesn't. I lean in to him. The smell has gone.

That is how it should be, but it never is. That is how I wanted it to be but it never was. A private moment captured on film for the world to see. But then it is not private but a commodity, my dad said. George says, Let it go. It's too late, I say, too late too late for what to stare death in the face it is never too late for that.

Do you need a ticket to get in? I ask. George says, not with me you don't. This, my friend, is my second home. He gets up and I follow him. Them photographs that you have seen with police at the gate, well I was one of them. We hung around to make sure he and his family stayed safe. You stay away from him Elvis, that's what I said, he says. I say, who? You know, the nigger man in the green tweed suit. He walked on but not me. I watched him open the big brass doors onto a great burning desire and it stops me in my tracks. I can see the flames climbing higher and higher and the station man with no eyes is laughing and singing at me and waving me in.

Now and then there's a fool such as I.

George walks on with arms outstretched. But I don't. I can't. I watch him beckon me in, smiling a big fat spider smile. I can't do it. My nerves tingle and my body's cold. I am walking on the King's grave.

I take in the air. I can smell a rose. The fat man is breathing down my neck. A dying wish, I say. I can't remember. I don't know you. You don't know me. I don't know me. Then it is not. What, a dying wish.

He grabs my arm and says; every breath you take every step you make, every move you make, I'll be watching you. I pull away and make my way back down the drive. I can feel him walking behind. He sings:

Old George Montgomery runs through the town; up Beale and down Main in his dark blue attire, tapping at the windows shouting through the locks are all the nigger men in bed because it's passed eight o'clock.

He whispers soft enough to wake the bees. I pick up the pace and repeat to myself, it's because everybody is scared.

There is nobody on the gate and no coaches across the street waiting to leave. I stop and turn and look back. The fat man and the King's mansion are not there and dark clouds are hanging low, threatening a storm. I wish Priscilla was here. I'd climb into her womb and feel safe. I am scared. The bogey men – the shadow men – are lurking, waiting. Dad, please I'm fifty-three, shall I go back the way I came? There is no going back son. Those bridges are burnt; turn left like I told you to all those many moons ago.

I turn left and cars are creeping like snails along wide, deserted concrete roads.

Hey little lady won't you come out tonight come out tonight come out tonight.

Lady of the night, I hear you calling, lady of the night, I hear you scream, don't hit me don't hit me there's a policeman watching; seriously there is a policeman watching. Seriously Dad, what did you expect a pat on the back a gold medal for your sins?

I'm on Winchester Street. I have missed my bus. The kids are in bed because it's passed eight o'clock and so is Lorrie but I don't know who with. The car parked up looks familiar. It's my dad's. I get close. The car door opens on the passenger side and she steps out adjusting her clothes and it's not my mam. Hey little lady won't you come out tonight. Hey little lady won't you come out tonight. I reach the crossroads of Highway 51 and Winchester Road. Across the way is a garage. My heart starts racing ten to the dozen. It is the gateway home I hope.

Behind the counter stands a very tall black guy wearing a bobble cap and wearing nothing else but a denim bib and brace cut of at the knees just like Tom did. Excuse me sir, I'm as polite as I can possibly be without embarrassing myself and he looks at me and screams, My my you are sight for sore eyes. You need gas? You need your car seeing to? You need something to eat? You sure look like you need something to eat. No sir, I say in a whisper. Stop saying sir, it ain't your place, he says to me. It's me that's supposed to be saying sir, he says. Don't you know the rules? You should know the rules by now, you being white annall and me being black. Where you from anyways? No, don't tell me. I'm good at this; youse from over the road, youse from that big ugly building on the hill over the road there, ain't I right? I've just come from there yes but I ain't from there no. Youse pulling my pisser mister or what, he says. No mister I ain't. That's better I like mister better than being called sir by a white mister with a quiff in his hair leaning the wrong way. Did you know it is leaning the wrong way? I just want you to tell me the way back, I say. The way back he says the way back from where? Downtown mister, I want to go Downtown where things will be great so they say. Oh, Downtown Beale and all that crap. Course, you one of them geezers celebrating his death, aren't you? No, not yet, I say with tongue in cheek.

You got a motor mister? You needs wheels man, to get to where you going, he says smiling. No I haven't, I say, fearing the worst. His jaw drops and his smile too. He screeches, Hold back the night please mister. His jaw drops closer to the floor and his smile disappears. You out here and you got no motor to your name. How do you think you goin' to get back home hey? cos it's there I guess, my man, is where you wanna be, am I right or am I wrong? It's the singer not the song, he whispers in my ear. I shake my head and say in return, No you're wrong, not the singer it was the song. He steps back and throws out his arms and shouts, I don't think so man, cos you look like shit. It's the shit of a dying man, it's in the eyes, fixed in a dead man's stare.

Something snaps and I scream, you got a problem with me son? Is it because you're black? Have you got a problem with that Jack? I just come here for help that is all. I stride towards him to show him the picture of Henry and the King. I get up close with my hand still in my pocket and he screams, don't shoot don't shoot, I was jacking you off man, that's all.

I take the photograph out of my pocket and hold it up close to his face. He steps back and I say, the black guy, in the picture, my friend, his name is Henry Fuller. I am looking for him. He has the answers I seek; the answers to my prayers you might say. You can say brother its okay, I'll take a look. He drops his hands and takes a look and laughs and says, so it is. It's old Henry with the man. Well I'll be damned and I thought he was dead. It's nineteen fifty-eight, I say. Well I'll be damned, and he looks at me smiling, yes I knows Henry, and you're a friend of his, you say? That's right. I put the photograph back and he shouts, TO Wilson you come out here, and beckons me to take it out again.

An older black man of about seventy-five, dressed in a dark suit and wearing a tie, comes out from behind a curtain and the tall young guy says to him TO you take a look at this photo that this here white fellow got, and he beckons me to show it to TO. What do think of that TO? Who would you say that is? And TO smiles, turns and walks back behind the curtain and the younger man tells me to put the photograph away and to go outside and I do what he says.

Outside TO Wilson's rotund face and frame is waiting for me in a battered old green Cadillac. He waves me to him and directs me to get in. I do and he pulls away. I tell him Beale Street and he doesn't answer so I'm not sure.

For how big these roads are, at least three lanes wide, there is not much moving traffic, only us going the other way. You know Henry then, TO? He doesn't take his eyes off the road and nods. This is good of you. I got pretty scared back there, thought I was lost didn't think I would get back tonight. I look at my watch and it is registering five thirty.

I've just been up there to that great big mansion on the hill but it didn't go well. I didn't step through the door. I left again. I don't know why TO. Well, I do. I saw the man with no eyes. Too much pain, I think. You think, he says. You don't know, then? I didn't belong I know that. Belong to what? he asks. I was with the fat man George Montgomery. He said he died beneath the Poplar tree. Do you know him? He told me to stay away from Henry. Why would he say that? I know why really. It's because he is black. George don't like black people. Do you believe in dreams T O? I've been getting a lot lately. I'm dying T O, you know. It is what we call the big C. Yes, if truth was known I shouldn't be here but hey.

TO says, what's with the limp? The limp, I reply I don't know. You don't know you limp? No, got used to it, I suppose. That's strange man. What me or the limp? Because I am not the only one who has a limp. That might be so brother, but you seem to be the only one that don't know he's got a limp. What's strange about that? It's my limp, been with me since I was a kid. They took the irons off when I was twelve. But you don't know why you got it? I don't know why people get hung up about it. I don't. Is one of your legs shorter than the other, is that it? It might be. Man you are not real, he says. Me? Not real? That is a laugh; that is a laugh and a half that is. No man this is a laugh and a half Ha! Ha! Ha! Ha...ha! Ha! That is a laugh and a half.

Are we there yet? Why you asking? I'm asking, if you must know, because, out there in the blackness, outside this dilapidated old car you are driving, I can't see any signs. I can't see anything at all in fact. Are you scared man? He asks. Scared? Of course I'm scared. I'm scared of death; I didn't think I would be but I am.

I was scared in sixty-eight, he says. In sixty-eight when it all began? He replies, In sixty-eight it all became real the whole shabam. When it was all turned upside down, you mean? In sixty-eight, black and white, they all started to listen, he shouts. It was never so black and white, I say, when they started listening to me. The black faces, I mean, they finally saw the sense in what I was saying. My old man didn't see the sense in any of it and my mother was too smitten.

After Echol and Robert died, I say, is that when it all started? You know about that? he asks. I've seen the photograph – Henry, Echol and Robert. Echol was Henry's friend. Henry took it hard. He thought the mayor would tell him what he wanted to hear but he didn't. Was that because he was the mayor? I say. Or was it because he was white? I told him what he wanted to hear but he didn't listen. Was that, TO, because you are black?

It was Mae Ray that turned him around. A good woman was Mae Ray. I say, A good-looking woman, I know that for a fact. Yeah, that's right, you and her have met. And he laughs, not a laugh and a half this time. Well, I think I did. She said it was her. But I can't be absolutely sure. I'm not sure of you, TO Wilson. You could be a figment of my imagination an image from a dream or a thought. I'm not absolutely sure about anything no more. Is that because nothing is as black and white as you imagined it to be before? I'm dying, that's all. Or I could be you, he says; now that's a thought. We are here. That will be fifty dollars please.

Fifty dollars for what, I shout. Take a look around you and see, he shouts. I don't have fifty dollars on me, I say. Oh but you have, he whispers low. I look deep into his face. It fills out even more. The tram lines disappear and his face is round and smooth like a babies bum. I see him properly now. It's the man from the stage. I dig deep into my trouser pocket and take out all the cash I have. That will do, and he takes it all. I haven't counted it, I say. No need, he says, I know the price you have to pay, and he smiles that rotund smile I saw cry on the stage the other day, the man who told me I was okay.

I look at my watch; it says five thirty, fifty dollars for no time at all. Did it seem like no time to you? No, it seemed longer. Then what is your gripe? You have paid me fifty dollars for a journey that seemed longer, who can argue with that? Was it short or was it long? Was it right or was it wrong? Who really knows? I don't, I say and give him the money I have in the palm of my hand and say, there you go. I don't know how much is there now we are even. Oh we can never be that, he says. I say, that might be a fact but I do know this for a fact too; this isn't Beale, it's Main. The car door opens on its own, leaving a tear in TO's eyes for two.

I step out of the car and say thanks. He drives away dropping my money out on to the street as he goes back to the future place. I scramble to pick it up but it all slips through my fingers and I watch it disappear down a hole in between the cobbles. Just like the marbles. You cheated George. I'm sorry Norm, but it was you who cheated on me.

I look at the buildings around me and I think I should be closer than this. I walk on not knowing one step from the next. It is dark and blacker clouds are still gathering. There is going to be some bad weather; you can smell it in the air. I see a café I recognise.

The same people dressed in their nightmare are sitting at tables next to the window like last time and facing me. I look them in the eye, they smile, I wave. The woman closest to me through the glass mouths: *Larry Payne is dead*. I smile and nod my head and tell her I know.

Norm asks, what you smiling at George? I wasn't smiling; the people in their fish bowl of a café were smiling at me. Well, they were smiling at you George because you were smiling at them. No Norm, they smiled at me first so, okay, I smiled back but I didn't know cos that's how it goes. You should know that.

George, I do because I have seen it before; you just don't know you are doing it. Remember that night in the pub? You had just been on stage and that guy with the curly hair and black face came over to you and asked you what you doing and you said you didn't know. You was smiling at his missus and he hit you and won. I told you Norm, I didn't know. Was it because, George, he was black and she was white? No Norm, you know why, she wasn't white she was my wife and I didn't know really that *Larry Payne was dead*. I told a lie, a whopping lie to save my skin.

My watch has stopped.

In the lift, I close my eyes until it stops. I get off and walk the corridor, the endless corridor with its naked magnolia walls, sheepishly eyeing a passer-by who is looking for the room he's forgot. On and on, round and round, nothing knowingly takes shape until a small room with white walls and black ugly machine lying still and asleep on the floor beckons me in by intentionally opening its jaws. I enter warily. Cohn is telling me to put on my blue suede shoes and walk *ten feet off the ground*. I have heard of such places pulling you in then spitting you out with you owing them. A wide screen TV above my head tells me of a coming storm. I am alone and facing a wall of glass *but do I really feel the way I do*. I do and walk through into an open concrete space that sits comfortably close to the night stars.

The open space is deathly quiet and littered with easy chairs. The night air is warm and surprisingly refreshing. It no longer matters. I am at ease. I am the giant with the building and streets below being mine for keeps. I walk the perimeter of my domain looking, touching, inspecting peering over the side leaning slightly, tempting fate and stopping, watching the minnows moving, toing and froing and I laugh out loud at the surprised look of wonder on the kids' faces below my bedroom window as they watch my Meccano pieces shower down around their feet, and then laugh even louder because they think it is God or even Santa Claus feeding their dreams.

I don't hear my dad come up the stairs and into my room. I don't feel his one, two, three slaps around my head and I don't hear him screaming venom in my ear because the laughter from below keeps out other voices, even those inside my head: *You what you what you what*, I scream, he says, You will pay the price. The cost, I say, is irrelevant it is just the theory of diminishing returns. Something he wouldn't and couldn't understand and why should he, he wasn't me.

I look down at my dad and watch him carefully and meticulously pick up every piece that lies on the barren cobbled street. He never says a word to the kids – I begged him not to – he just looks up and points to the sky. Not even when Norman is insisting that it was an act of God and the pieces belong to them. We are, he says, the chosen ones. I can see my dad walking back into the house grinning. I watch him and cry. Norman never knew the truth of it. I sit now and watch my dad leave with his drinking coat on, whistling:

Green door what's that secret you're keeping

And I hear James Cagney scream: *top of the world, Ma*. Then George Montgomery shoots him.

Like me at the top of the world close to the dancing stars, the bright glittering stars hanging low and loose. Ladies and gentlemen the winner is Elvis Presley, and I take a bow and my mam claps and Norman is clapping too and Priscilla is clapping and

Henry is clapping and I show Henry his photo and Henry points at the King, smiles and says He was my friend he truly was, but he never knew, no he never knew what Memphis was, where its soul was hidden. He came like me just to sing and he sang, but he could never touch its soul. No sir, Echol touched its soul then got crushed in the back of a garbage truck. Robert just smiled he didn't know what else to do even with mangled brains he smiled that's why we had to fight. The King never understood because all he wanted to do was sing and sometimes son that just ain't enough. No sir, it just makes the singing soulless if all you want to do is sing; it just isn't enough.

I sit down in an easy chair and take out the photograph. Now I have two. Henry, you are looking like you're deep in thought. Standing on a picket line takes a lot of thinking about George. We are watching Memphis white folk: men, women with their little children walk by with their banners screaming at us loud and clear to get back to work nigger youse ain't fit to wipe my nose, and I am thinking nothing's changed I am still a man and that's all we ask. To be treated the same as you. I am a man and I drift away. Someone is gently shaking me free. I open my eyes and the stars have been replaced by a blue clear heavy sky.

Have you been here all night? Priscilla asks and I shield my eyes from the warm sun so I can see her face. She has the photograph in her hand. Please, and I hold my hand out and she gives it to me. I thank her and try to get up out of the chair but fail. I feel her arms go under mine and I brush her away and try again, and again I fail. Fatigue, I say. Go tell it to the Indians, she says and turns to leave. I turn in my chair and see her at the door. The white walled room is rocking; Cohn sings about ghosts he saw on Union Avenue. I shout her back and apologise. I feel exhausted. I don't have the strength to move and my back hurts. She gets a chair and sits down beside me.

I pass her the photograph. I watch her slide a finger gently and slowly across the image. He hasn't changed. I say, He has his eyes on the world not the other two. She says, they know what is coming. She passes it back and leans back in her chair taking in the sun. I do the same. It is the right thing to do for us both.

I close my eyes and hear Marc walking with heavy shoes down Beale. THUD THUD THUD ten feet off the ground and I drift underground with the THUD

THUD THUD of the hydraulic hammer banging in my ear as it crashes through the seams of endless coal.

We are sitting watching and wondering if the roof is going to hold then the news comes through that they are closing the pits. The hammering stops, the men stop, the cage comes down and we go up and out. Out into the blinding sun and stand firm like a brick wall but not me. I'm off to chase my dream.

Then my poor dad becomes a brick wall all by himself, a solid lump of pride that, like the Greek fellow, he pushes up and then down and through endless heart breaking days and we stand and watch and I sing the song. The song binds him tight to his rock. I keep singing and the rock keeps rolling and then the fat lady dies and the rock stops. Just long enough for the furnace to swallow the fat lady up, spit her out as dust and the dust to be packed away tightly in a little red holy red jug. Amen, he says, and goes back to his rock and starts pushing again but not before he gives me the note that the fat lady wrote without a word said. I would love you to be in Memphis Tennessee singing the songs that he sang. So I came alone, just me and the big C and holy dust, afraid, heaving my own rock through Henry's home. I'll help you carry it, she says.

My eyes open up to the burning sun and I ask, why? You talk in your sleep, she says and I say, Yes that might be the case but you owe me nowt so why now? I'm focused, focused enough to haul myself up onto my feet and walk. Priscilla does the same and follows me out. You are half my age and I was once fat with a limp so why do you stay? I have to, she says, it's my job, and she laughs.

She is laughing when we enter my room. I made a promise, she says as I climb in to the shower and she laughs some more; her laughter cascades all over my body and settles right at my core and I cry again, deep cries that move the earth. Someone once said to me that crying makes you fat. I don't know who but if it was true then I should be as fat as a pig.

Now I'm dry and dressed and in the room and I ask her a promise to whom? Shall we go to Lauderdale today? She asks. I tell her I've been to Graceland but I couldn't go in, what makes you think Lauderdale will be any different? Because, she says, you will be with me and not the fat man. I will not hurt you like the fat man can and the fat man can ask Henry. Shall we have breakfast first? She asks.

We sit at the window overlooking the Mississippi. The sun looks hot as it glistens on its centre. She has toast and I have eggs sunny side up. I ask her, Have you ever read *Tom Sawyer*, and she answers in a Southern drawl, I knows Tom Sawyer, and we both laugh and I answer back, in a Southern drawl, The greatest book that there ever was, and we both laugh again only this time Priscilla laughs louder then goes into a whisper and leans in towards me and says, I knows Huckleberry Finn too.

She leans back relaxed in her chair like a young Southern dame and chews on her toast and says, I was once in love with Huck but he wasn't in love with me. He never fell in love with anybody he just up and left and nobody seen him again. Her hair is a different colour now – mousy like my mam's.

We leave the hotel together and walk down Market Avenue and past St Mary's Catholic Church until we come to Lauderdale with its gates secured tight against the outside world. I can't see any other way in. It is like Fort Knox, my dad would say. Priscilla takes my hand and leads me to a big clump of overgrown shrubbery. She squeezes through it without effort. No, I say, not me. You got to be joking. I stand stiff, reluctant to move. Now she's gone.

I step back and try and find a gap big enough but there isn't one. The tunnel of love, I laugh to myself whilst I whisper her name then shout it out loud. She doesn't answer. I am not surprised, neither would I.

I suppose I should panic but I don't. In fact, I feel indifferent to it all: this, her. I walk back the way we came determined to rid myself of it all. But my limping leg begins to ache. She could be lying unconscious in a hole. I go back but cannot find the exact spot. I turn back again but my leg hurts even more. This time I walk away. Shit bugger arsehole I don't care. Then out of nowhere a gap appears. I bend down and look through.

Is everybody ready? Okay, roll the camera and action! She is sitting on a step talking and laughing with a couple of young men – one acned with fair hair, holding a guitar looking scared and lost in time singing about a dog that has gone to heaven – and the other is me twelve and proud. And there it is as clear as day. I see it now and cut it's a wrap. She is not mine she is every man's. I leave.

There is a skip in my step as I walk back down Market Avenue. It doesn't matter anymore I tell myself. I feel relieved. I cross over and walk towards St Mary's Catholic Church, a brown imposing building that sits awkwardly amongst scattered small private industries. *There she goes baby here am I.* It doesn't matter anymore. I've done it and I've seen it, I can say that now. Don't make me laugh. Say it to whom? I hear you say. There is Hank.

Hank will put me right. Hank will listen. Hank, my old friend, I have to go. Oh sir, ain't that a shame leaving so soon. Do not kid me none man, I'll say. Now I see the two young men from the steps driving towards me. They are in a battered old grey pickup truck. The faired haired acned one is strumming his guitar and singing loud enough for me to hear. *If there is a heaven there's one thing I know.* Priscilla is sitting between them. There is a loud bang and she's gone gone gone.

Now Henry is ahead of me and in front of him, crawling and chugging along the well-worn cobbled street of my youth, is an old battered sanitation truck. Henry is swinging trash cans across its back with ease. A strong smell of fish and rotting meat permeates the air. I shout, Henry knock on the green door and say hello. My mam and dad will be there. But he doesn't hear. I try and get closer but the heavy pounding rain and the whining of the old truck is holding me back. I hear men screaming, Get me out, and set us free, dear lord God please set us free. The rain and the truck stop. Henry drops the can and runs to the back and climbs into the trucks devouring jaw. My gammy leg is stuck to the tar in the road and my feet are devoid of shoes. I open my mouth and scream a silent Henry! I watch a wall of coal collapse and swallow bodies and he is there behind the dust pushing a heavy boulder through the tunnel of love. There is no point, they win every time. It doesn't matter son, you still got to try cos you don't know whose watching.

My mam is sitting in the corner of the mine on her brand new settee shouting through a cloud of dust *The King! The King!* Choking on my own blood I'm silently screaming, Henry! Please help me. Henry whispers, from a distance off George give us a song, George, give us a song. A choir of floating strangled faceless voices join in the chorus: Georgie, Georgie give us a song give us a song give us a song.

Henry! Please can I come with you in the ambulance? I need to come with you in the ambulance because somebody has stolen my shoes. I won't be a nuisance I promise. Mam, I'm going with Henry. Dad, Henry's black. So am I son, so am I.

Are you happy George? I'm happy nurse. Nothing is broken, you just wasn't with us for a while. My eyes open and a new smiling face is looking down at me. I feel something soft under my body. Hello sir. Where am I? You are in hospital. Why, did I collapse again? You've collapsed before? Well, not collapsed I fainted, heat exhaustion, heat exhaustion in February?

She is wearing a white coat and her hair is grey and tucked up neatly under a small white cap, but she hasn't an old face. Yes sir, it's the first of February today and it's raining. I need to take your name. Can I leave? She has a seductive smile. You can sir, soon as we get back your x-ray. What happened to me? A car knocked you down. Was it the fat man? She laughs quietly. I don't know whether the person driving the car was fat or not, sir. Apparently you stepped out into the road. Someone said they thought you did it deliberately. Did what deliberately, I ask. She said, stepped out, into the road, in front of the car that knocked you down. Good job it wasn't going any faster than it was, hey sir? She is taking my pulse. Did you do it deliberately sir?

Step in front of the car on purpose? Her hand feels cold round my wrist. Did I try and kill myself you mean? Yes sir, I do mean that.

Momentarily I can't answer because I don't know. I could have been trying to top myself but I don't know. In fact, I cannot remember any of it. Well, the woman says you did. She was alongside you when you stepped into the road suddenly, she says. What woman, what did she look like? Oh, she was about thirty years of age. She had a bob cut and was wearing a duffle coat. Blue was it? Yes sir, I think it was. Did she have two young children with her one about seven and the other about three? No she didn't. In fact, that is why she is not with you now. She came with you in the ambulance but had to leave. She said she had to pick the children up from your mother's. Lorrie. Pardon sir. Did she say her name was Lorrie? Yes, I think she did.

She puts my arm back down gently on to the bed, leans over me, pulls down the skin under both eyes and peers in. She smells of peaches. She whispers, Interesting. I whisper back, is it dark in there? She straightens up. I see her eyes searching for an answer.

There doesn't seem to be any identification on you. And you can tell that by looking into my eyes can you? So I need to know who you are. And you cannot tell that by looking at me, then? I need you to tell me. My name is...my name is... something is not working right... my name is... Do you know where you are? Yes in what looks like... and I search the room for an answer... a hospital bed. Is this it, is this what it has all come down to in the end? What sir? This, me, death. She smiles and cocks her head to one side like a curious dog.

Have I reached the final curtain?

We are joined by a man in a blue Italian-cut mohair suit carrying an x-ray. He has dark brown hair cut in the Beatles style. Good day Mr Proctor, the nurse says to him. Good day Miss Ratchett, you're looking nice. Do you fancy a drink later I know a nice secluded place where we can dance and sing. He holds the x-ray up to what little light there is smiles and points his finger at a spot on the x-ray and says to Miss Ratchett, we can go there where there are a few grey areas, he says. I know that place, I reply. Yes, he says, it is where there are little vermin helping themselves to your insides, he says smiling. Ironic really, I say, when you know they will only finish up eating themselves like we all do in the end, so if there is nothing else can I go? I presume you are insured? Nurse Ratchett asks with a grin that would shame a pussy cat. What against death, are you? I say. And the mohair man laughs and says sarcastically, Typical is that, you were always the same, and walks away with nurse what's-her-face on his arm.

The room is clinically white with empty old iron beds scattered around. An injun sits perched high on a window sill still as a mouse holding a single white magnolia flower in his hand. He nods his head and I nod mine and we say Hi in unison. He shouts Welcome to the cuckoo's nest, and I say Thanks, how are you today? He says, I'm not going to let them see.

I ease myself, with the aid of the side of the bed, down to the floor. I am on all fours searching for my shoes. They are not there, a voice says. I look up and Henry, in his green tweed suit, is standing with a wheelchair. He says, Get in and don't say a word. I'm your porter for the day. I didn't know you worked here, I say. No, he replies you don't, do you.

He takes a white sheet from the bed, puts it around me and pushes me towards a door like a ghost. The injun waves the magnolia at me and the flower falls to the floor. Good luck, Randle, he screams. What you doing here Henry, I ask from under the sheet. Henry doesn't answer me and pushes me through swing doors. Nurse Ratchett is standing at a reception desk fiddling with her desk. She smiles as we pass. She was right it is raining.

We turn left and hurry towards a car that is parked in the last bay. As far away as possible, I say. I get out and struggle to get to the car; my feet are wet and freezing cold. Henry helps me in to the passenger seat. He leaves the chair where it is, gets in and we drive off.

I fall asleep and see the fat man standing on the steps of Graceland watching me leave. It was wrong, I scream in my sleep. I couldn't do it. I couldn't do it. You couldn't do what? Go in Henry, the flames, the burning love, it didn't seem right. I wake up looking at him looking at me. I want my shoes. I want to go home. Don't worry George, we will be there soon.

I want to go home Henry. You can't, not yet. I don't answer. I just stare up at the green interior of the car roof. I need shoes. I've got shoes, he says. No, my own shoes I mean. The ones I stepped off the plane in. Where are we going? Home, eventually, he says.

You know I had never been on a plane before. Lorrie tried to persuade me once that it was the right thing to do, her me and the kids too. But I could never see the point. She never tried to persuade me again. Now they've gone alone to I don't know where.

I ain't ever had kids. Me and Mae Ray had an understanding. Life was just too unfair. We didn't want to raise kids in a plantation city. Now we've stopped. Henry gets out of the car and beckons me to follow. I told you I have no shoes. You don't need shoes where we are going. I get out and follow and the ground is soft like a carpet and he stops between two graves. The rain has stopped. One of them reads: Echol and the other Robert that is all. No surname none at all. Why? I ask. He says, Work it out, and he takes me to a third and says that's mine. Yours, I gasp. Yes sir Echol and Robert and Henry Fuller together at last. My bare feet are getting colder.

Henry turns round and walks back to the car. I watch him get in, start up the engine and drive away back the way we came. I stand frozen to the spot telling myself he will be back but he doesn't come back and the ground now is wet and hard. I tiptoe back to where the car was standing and on the cracked, narrow road is a pair of battered pit boots. Inside one is a note: Put these on. They will keep you warm. Love Dad. They fit like a glove. I tighten them up and walk away from the field with three graves or was it four.

I walk and I walk through the cold dark quiet night for ages it seems. Thinking only of what I've seen: an open grave. Suddenly there is an ear-piercing noise that opens up the ground beneath my feet and I stumble and fall. I grope around feeling my way, trying to make sense of it all. I feel hard walls each side and something slimy and small is crawling over me. I scream a quiet scream for help. I realise now what Henry meant, why he brought me here, it is here where I am going to die. Am I home I wonder?

They say that the first thing to go is your sight and the last thing is your hearing. They are right because although I cannot see a bloody thing, just feel the creepy crawlies eating the inside of me I hear a man singing my favourite song. The voice gets closer and closer and buries itself inside my brain. I scream for it to stop. It does. I force my eyes to look up at the moon looking down on me. Then it half disappears and is replaced by a shadowy figure standing doing the same. My eyes focused I see it is George Montgomery dressed for work.

He bends down and helps me up and asks me if I am okay. I straighten up, brush myself down and try and start all over again and George laughs.

I look at him and ask him why he is dressed like he is: all shiny and blue. Like this? He says. Well, it is because I'm a cop, dummy, or are you taking the piss? Ain't I seen you somewhere before, he asks. I shrug my shoulders with uncertainty but still say, of course you have George, I'm Elvis Presley, remember. And before I could explain, as if I really wanted to, he has my head locked tight under his arm. I am frantically trying to pull myself free watching our feet dance round an uncovered grave waiting for the moment he is going to throw me in. Please let me go, I choke.

He lets me go and asks me if I was one of them civil rights loonies from up North. I tell him through unwanted tears, No I'm from England. Okay, you'd better come with me. You are not safe round here on this side of town. Too many dark featured creatures hanging around waiting for people like you and me, if they get the chance, if you know what I mean. Where you staying man? I'm on a visit I forget, I reply. My head hurts, I say also but I don't know why. I'm not surprised; he says sympathetically, it was a nasty fall. Come with me, he turns and walks heavily to a blue and white sparkly clean Chevrolet and I follow. I have a blanket in the car to keep you warm, he says. I say to his back, I'm looking for the King. We get into his car. Him in the front and me in the rear and I wrap the blanket round and he asks, what's with the limp? Leg been attacked has it? Sought of, I reply.

So where is your coat? Got any ID? I'm confused. Sorry, I reply. I feel in my trouser pockets no nothing at all only the photo I must keep hidden. Robbed in the process, he looks at me and smiles and says, Welcome to Memphis man. We drive off to who knows where.

You called me George back there, he said. I say, you look like a George I thought I knew you and I thought you knew me too. And why would I know you? He asks. I don't know myself or even my own wife and we've been married ten years. What's her name? I say. Why do you ask? Oh, just passing the time of day. Well if you must know it's Lorraine and we got two kids.

I don't recognise the streets. The buildings we pass have broken windows and remnants of wood and glass lie unattended in the road. There are no cars or people passing. I ask the back of his head, what has happened here?

We've a bit a bother, he says in a matter of fact way. The black folk of our city are trying to grab for themselves their own claim to fame. Communists and agitators from up North are leading the way getting the black workers all riled up over nothing, wanting them to join some union or other, but Mr Mayor won't stand for it, no sir and neither will we. We intend to put a stop to it in fact. The law is on our side and they are breaking it. It is as simple as that. If you cross the law you pay the price. My daddy taught me that. That's how it is in a civilised country and Memphis is that if nothing else, he says. And he says further, I could have been a singer you know. I've got the voice so my mamma said, God bless her soul. It's what killed her, you know, me not following my dream. Her name was Lorraine too, something in that I suppose. So you're looking for the King. Why?

I want to say I don't know but I don't. Instead what pours out of my mouth is: I think I want to kill him. You think, he says, smiling at me through his mirror. The words fall out uncontrollably. Yes, I'm dying and I think he should die too. I won't be free if I don't. Sort of resolution, you might say. A cleansing of the soul, he says, quite right too and I can help. And he laughs. And I laugh too. And the laughs merge into one big hoot. And I ask him how he knew.

We are crawling from one dark street to another. Black bin bags and bins spill over inviting black brown rats as big as your arm to feast on what remains on the bloodied concrete roads where once I felt jolly feet pounding out songs worth their salt.

Armageddon my friend, the fat man says-it's that word again- and he suddenly stops the car with a jolt. The King is in town stirring their souls and that ain't right, no sir, so it has to be stopped for good, if you know what I mean. We sit waiting for something to happen.

The rain comes down in buckets bouncing off the car like bullets. Got to do something with you man, he says. I can't let you walk the streets of my beloved Memphis like some crazy stray. I'm not crazy, I say, that is one thing I know I'm not. A figure of speech mister, that's all; a figure of speech. But you got to admit, looking like you do now, you don't inspire confidence. You got no money and no identification; you look like you've been living underground for eternity and died with your pit boots still on. I stare at myself through the window on a dark background and agree.

I'll take you down to the station and let you wash up. We might even have a change of clothing for you. I bet a nigger your size has just died and he laughs. The Crown you say. I don't think I did.

No sir, there ain't no hotel in Memphis by that name. Could be one over the bridge in Arkansas or up the road in Nashville but there certainly isn't one called that here. Could it be the Peabody? That is where most white folk stay that is not from around here. It doesn't sound right, I reply. I say the first thing that comes into my head. I think it is a boarding house on Main, I say rather too excitedly, opposite the Lorraine? Young Morrow owns it Number four two two. That is interesting, he says. Okay, lets us get you cleaned up and fed then we can work out your destiny.

The last time I was in the back of a police car we were searching the streets looking for the three lads that had beaten me up over a girl that wasn't mine but a Canadian man's who drove the number 53 bus. I was black and blue with bruises the size of tattoos that cover your arm and chest. My dad got involved and insisted, in the only way he knew how, that we track down the insidious disease. His words not mine. So we cruised at about ten miles an hour round well known places with me wishing I was back home in my bed.

Then we saw them standing on the corner of Salisbury Street watching all the girls go by. And my dad pointed and screamed and I shouted back for all the world to hear No that's not them. The consequences would have been worse than the beating if I had agreed, if you know what I mean, and you should do by now.

George hands me a green check shirt and I put it on. Don't worry he says, he is nearly dead, and I ask him, Black or white, and he says, It is not a bad fit what do you think? I keep on the same trousers and boots. Do you know his name? I ask. Robert I think. Okay, you ready? What am I supposed to do now? I ask. You come with me and stick close. That is not what I meant.

At the car he tells me to sit in the back and I do what he asks without question. Then he speaks, my mammy was afraid of the dark in her later years. She wouldn't go out when the light had disappeared. There are too many bad people out there she would say too many goblins and witches eying you up. I would laugh and she'd get annoyed and say, I've seen them George, you mark my words, lurking out there, and she'd point at the window. They are waiting for me see. I tell your dad but he just laughs like you and after me, they will come for you. So you count your blessings George that is all I can say. It could have been me talking to him. But I'm not sure if it wasn't

I ask the man in front where he lives and he says Germantown. We've only just moved there. We lived over near Highway 51 but it got a bit noisy if you know what I mean; cars driving up and down all day and all night long. It'll be worse now there is a new addition to the family, everybody around there wanting to take a peak. Nice he is in Beverley Hills working on a new film away from all this, you know what I mean. No I don't I say. He says, Lisa Maria. The new baby is called Lisa Maria.

Hey there are a couple of English guys working alongside the mayor perhaps you are one of them. I don't think so, I say. How do you know? You took a bang on the head remember. Perhaps your name is Crown, Mister Crown. I didn't say crown you did. That might be so but you don't know do you? I'll take you over to meet him. He'll be interested in what you told me. I can't remember what I told him. It seems such a long time ago and he rambles on.

I can't understand for the life of me why they have turned on him like they have. Who? I ask quietly, I just want to sleep. His family treated them well. I bet you a flea's eye to squirrel's fanny that you're one of them. A flea's eye, a squirrel's fanny, I bet you I'm not, I say under my breath.

So tomorrow morning, my friend, you and me, bright and early, will go over to the city hall and straighten all this out. I bet you a flea's eye to a squirrel's fanny. I say half consciously, I'm not your friend. What time is it now? I barely ask and he says,

April 3rd nineteen sixty-eight. And I say are you for real and he replies you tell me brother it's your shout.

The chatter has stopped and the sign reads Main Street North. Through hazy light outside we crawl pass the city hall and bodies wearing masks spraying stuff over rotting garbage from canisters that fit snugly on their backs. Pesticide, the voice in front shouts maggots everywhere. Fucking unions we do not want them here. These niggers are his children you know and he feels betrayed after all what he has done for them, he says. And I agree. But I don't know why perhaps to save my own skin. He's feeling let down and hurt. Don't you agree? He asks. I nod my head. It is the easiest thing to do; the talking inside my head is beginning to hurt.

He turns into Beale and a bomb's been dropped it seems. He repeats, Armageddon see. They even eat up their own. Can you understand that because I certainly don't? It's about right and wrong George, my dad would say and the man in front asks, what's that? It is not just about winning it's about taking part, I say and my name is Elvis Presley. Yeah right, he laughs, and mine's Priscilla. You might be, I say nonchalantly. It certainly isn't Henry.

He stops the car. The rain is flying about like bullets. They don't even respect tradition, he says pointing his finger to a building outside the car I can barely see called Schwabs: *Better goods at lower prices*. It has its windows out. Its shelves are bare but for a smattering of trinkets. The sign should read: *Better goods at no prices*. He turns the engine off and we wait *for hell to freeze* what seems like ages and then it happens. The rain stops.

I see three black men walk towards the car. The fat man gets out with truncheon at the ready and faces them. Two black men run off and leave one behind. I close my eyes tight and slide down the seat hoping for sleep. It rains again and the car door opens, two this time one each side and one voice gets in cursing the rain and it sounds like Henry. I sit up and he turns and winks as the car starts up and leaves. What are you doing here, I ask. He replies, you put me here you tell me. I watch him turn on the radio. The Beatles sing:

He's a nowhere man, sitting in his nowhere land, making all his nowhere plans.

And he sings:

Doesn't have a point of view, doesn't know where he is going to, isn't he a bit like you and me.

And we crawl up Beale passed a battered Lansky's shop and turn right onto Main. You can't get any blacker than that one, don't you agree? And Henry nods his head and says:

Listen to the rhythm of the pouring rain. Telling me what a fool I've been.

The car stops outside a florist shop. Mae Ray's name is above the door.

I wish that it would go away and let me cry again.

The withered magnolia flowers behind the glass are choking on their tears. George Montgomery turns off the engine and gets out of the car. He goes around to the back and lifts a green holdall out of the boot that has Memphis Redbirds written on it. It is raining sheets. He goes to the front entrance of the florist and opens the door. Henry turns to me and sings:

And let me be alone again my friend.

George Montgomery walks in. He is gone a few seconds. I ask Henry what is happening but he doesn't answer. He is sobbing instead. And I sob too and our sobbing morphs into one big sob and we watch George Montgomery walk out into the rain and beckon me over. The sobbing stops and Henry has gone leaving me to face myself alone, alone there is a song there somewhere if only I could remember. I go to him and follow him without question up a flight of stairs and into a small room. The green bag is against a white wall. The room has four white walls and an iron hospital bed. He walks to me standing by the side of the bed and says you can stay here tonight and gives me a bear hug longer than I think necessary. He smiles and says: for what you are about to do may the lords be truly thankful. He turns and leaves the way he came. I hear his footsteps trip trotting down the stairs and the door slams to.

It is silent but for the rhythm of the pouring rain outside the window of the bathroom opposite the bed. Is this where I am going to die, I wonder. Now Mr Proctor get into bed if you don't mind; it's late. But can I have a look first please nurse through the window at the flashing light. I think I have been here before, and she smiles that beautiful Priscilla smile and says, I don't think, I know. Go on then but don't take too long you have got a long day ahead of you. Doctor King is doing his rounds and you know he doesn't like to be kept waiting. Okay then I won't peep, and I get on to the bed. It is the Lorraine Motel, she says, that is where the doctor is staying, and then I think I fall asleep but who knows about these things I certainly don't anymore.

I have a dream for sale. Who will buy my dream for sale?

The fat man is leaning against the white wall unzipping the green holdall that weighs a ton. I lifted it up whilst everybody else was asleep. I crept out of bed unseen. What you got in it, my wife? He laughs and takes out a rifle new and unseen and hands it to me. What do you want me to do with this? Doctor King is in town. I know, I say, I am seeing him tomorrow. Then he has to be stopped, he says, don't you think? A better bedside manner is to be desired but beyond that... I thought you wanted to see him dead, he says angrily now, get on with it, and he throws the rifle onto the bed. Or else. I scream at him, or else what as he slams the door and on the stairs he shouts back, you will die with no soul if you don't.

There is a knock on the door. I open my eyes. I tell myself to listen to the rhythm of the pouring rain and it will go away but it doesn't it knocks again and says my name whatever that is. The door opens and standing there is the tall lanky black man from the café. He says I have been thinking about what we were talking about and I want to know: why did he not sing man when he was in Prestwick one song man that's all one song that's all it would have took to set things on its way just like you did the other day anyways Henry sent me, he says smiling. He told me to take you to him. He couldn't come himself because he is driving the car. I say, Is it that time already? And I walk to him. Don't forget your green bag, he says. Oh that, I reply. It don't matter it will still be there when I wake up and he laughs and we leave.

The rain is lashing down and I run to the corner of Mulberry where Henry is waiting. He tells me to get in the back and I tell him to bollocks and get into the driving seat. I tell him I am tired of taking a back seat so I put Henry there instead and Henry laughs and shouts at last at last.

The car door opens and a round-faced black man with a slight moustache and wearing a smart dark suit gets in beside him. Henry tells me that it is Doctor King and I say, I know it is it is me who has put him there it is my dream remember. Now I feel I am staring death in the face. And I'm feeling good. I drive off feeling totally in control.

The two men in the back are talking about the meeting to come and about Doctor King's flu and about how he asked Mr Abernathy to take the meeting tonight because he didn't feel right but Mr Abernathy kept insisting he came to the hall because it was packed to the brim with black faces expecting to see Doctor King sing and I ask, What about me. Do I get to sing again? And they both laugh and Henry says, I've granted you your wish man here is the King the rest is up to you.

I turn left onto the long drive *home*. See, I say, I do know the way. Through the rain and the mist the Poplar tree weeps green tears. George sits beneath it sheltering from life. He waves as we pass by. I don't wave back. At the top of the steep climb I turn the car engine off. The two lions sit proud guarding the steps waiting in anticipation for the other King to appear. I know this because it is my dream and I am desperate to make this happen. Two for the price of one, Henry says, literally with his tongue in his cheek.

The doctor coughs and sneezes, looks at his watch and asks Henry if it's going to happen. Henry tells him it's not my call it's his. I say, Coughs and sneezes spread diseases, and like magic the door to the mansion opens and Paul Simon sings: *Saw the ghost of Elvis on*

Union Avenue followed him up to the gates of Graceland then I watched him walk right through.

My dad said, George you will not get anywhere because you have no ambition, and I say, what is that when it's at home? Drive son, something to aim for something worthwhile not this. But I am on a drive. A big long drive and who got me here? Me. Yes but you just sit and wait George, sit and wait in somebody else's shadow.

And there it is son there it is. The very thing you have been waiting for coming your way so what will it be. I see it Dad, it walks with a limp and is five foot five tall and it's me.

Henry and the man with the tache laugh and I turn and look death in the eye and it winks. We all wink back and leave. Did death know it was me? I shut my eyes tight and open them again hoping to wake up from the dream.

I am in the rain standing alone. The doctor with the tache and Henry have gone. The road ahead is crowded with black faces all happy in song.

Ain't gonna let nobody turn me around turn me around turn me around keep on walking keep on talking cos I'm marching on the people's land.

I am walking but not talking because none of the black faces know I'm there, just me. The cobbled street is lined with houses all with green doors and I walk past Norman and my mam waving to me. I wave back at my dad standing at the bedroom window crying for peace and there it is ahead of me the Temple tall where the black man in the dark suit will sing.

And the round-faced black man with the moustache and smart black suit is standing high in the sky looking down on a sea of black faces craning their hearts and necks to listen to him singing their song about the nation being sick and of Negroes going round scratching where they didn't itch and laughing when they weren't being tickled and the mayor being in need of a doctor and sanitation workers being in need of support.

And I am feeling numb, confused, abandoned in a world I don't understand and there because some black person that I don't know from Adam wants me there. I feel alienated in a timeline that I can only remember as the turning point in my life when the man I idolised got onto a stage in a tight-fitting leather suit not a year after this one song was sung, not in some artificial studio a long way from home, but from high on a mountain top too high for me to reach.

Well I don't know what will happen now; we've got some difficult days ahead. I have looked over the edge and I have seen the Promised Land.

Henry is standing next to me. He isn't joining in with the hollering and the singing and the cheering. He is standing still amongst the swaying and the stamping with a look of detachment on his face. I cannot will him to move. Leave me alone, I say. I shut my eyes tight and open them again and I wake up on Willoughby Street near where I live outside Henry's house. I tell him I know a girl on Willoughby Street I wonder if she is in. Lorrie her name is and she has two kids.

He says, I can't believe George, I can't believe. Mae Ray says, Believe in the King, believe in him if there is nothing else to believe in. We sit at his small table facing each other staring closely at each other's face. I can't believe it's me and I can't believe I'm him. I try hard, he says, but something inside just gets in the way. I know what it is its Robert and Echol they are to blame. I know and Norman too and my mam and my dad and Lorrie, the kids and Uncle Tom Cobley and all: everybody else but me and you. Everybody but me and you are at fault for feeling the way we do. I feel intoxicated by it all. This, I believe, is the moment everything else has been leading up to. Put the dream aside. Put the dream aside. Wake up to reality.

Do you remember that American television series about a man who is sent back to different periods in history in order to change things. He was sent back to get things back on track so history can pan out as we have known it to be. Is that what's happening to you and me Mr Draper. Have we reached that point where we can shout Eureka now I have got it all down on paper for us to believe it is true? *I Am A Man;* what does it mean in the end Mr Draper for you?

What does it mean Elvis, or is it George? Does one think one way and the other another? Who is the wicked witch in this scenario hey? Is it Mae Ray or my mother? Or is it both. A black and white witch like the story goes. Does the King really have to die? I love Mae Ray but she is in the way. This is Henry talking now, keep up if you can. This is his lament not mine, I think.

We wouldn't have got paid if we had gone home while it rained so they sat in the back of the truck till it stopped but it didn't. I said I would drag the garbage cans off the posh people's drives and in the meantime they could rest in the back but the driver didn't know that. I heard the sound of the hydraulics that moves the big plates that mash up the garbage and they mashed up Robert and Echol instead. Put the dream away. Henry screams, is this the truth? Is this all there is? I wake with a thumping head in the room I was in before.

I raise myself up onto my elbows and I am on the same bed with its plain blue sheet dragging on the floor. Daylight throws a shadow onto the white wall and I notice the green holdall has gone. I ease myself up onto my feet and walk into the bathroom and have a pee into a brown stained bowl beneath a peeling open window. This is not my bathroom. The rain has stopped. A saxophone is playing a tune the King sings and loves.

I am tired I am weak I am lost.

The sweet joy of relief is suddenly replaced by a loud noise that near busts my ears and I look up from the stream and I see a round-faced, black man with a tache and dressed in a dark suit, lying on the floor of a balcony coughing and sneezing up blood that belongs to him outside an open green door. Smart suited black men are leaning over him pointing up at me. There, they scream in unison, the cripple, up there he's the one to blame that's him.

I duck down the best I can and lock away what is left of me and make for the main door. I hear footsteps running down the stairs and I shout, Is that you? And the voice shouts back, grab the bag and follow me. I grab the bag that once wasn't there and charge down the stairs and into the street. A car sits waiting with its engine running and its door open and the voice beckons me in. I jump onto the back seat struggling to breathe. The voice beside me says, well done, job done. Now let's go.

He drives down Main at high speed and in control. We have to get to a safe place, the voice behind me says. Where is that, I say, there is no such thing as a safe place; they will get you wherever you are. The voice beside me laughs then goes quiet.

I got this idea in my head we were going to see the man in charge, I say to the voice next to me. You said he would be able to tell me who I was and what I was doing here. You said he was the one with all the right answers. But that shouldn't worry you now, the voice replies. Anyway he'll be running round like a headless chicken getting things into place. What is that?

I ask. Oh, you know this and that the ins and outs of it all. His head is all over the place. Like mine, I say.

It laughs some more again while it speaks you're a strange one, it says. Me, why? I ask. We know that you killed the King. No, no not me I haven't killed anybody not me. Calm down Mr Proctor, don't get stressed you did what you said you wanted to do and that's good. What I wanted to do was sing my song. Be sure what you are wishing for you said to the nigger me and the others that inhabit your world.

We all understand, we all sympathise; you did what you had to do. You have sung your song; you have put your demons to rest now there is just one more thing before you leave. What is that? I ask myself. And I pass the big white gates and drive up to the mansion on the hill and Paul sings:

And my travelling companions are ghosts and empty sockets I'm looking at ghosts and empties

The proud stone lions have gone. I take a key out of my pocket and put it into the lock. I saw him last night and it laughs some more and Paul sings:

But I have reason to believe we will be received in Graceland.

I walk in and the lights are off and it's freezing cold.

I have spent my life, since I was twelve, taking care of the King. I have stood tall and proud defending his name. Now here I am with all my ghosts and empty rooms with death sitting snuggly in the palm of my hand like the eyes of the station host. They are all here, my shadows, my ghost sitting round my iron bed in my cold white walled room waiting for me to disappear. I sit on an old rocking chair that was once my Nan's and sway backwards and forwards to the rhythm of the tune that is playing in my head and Paul sings: *And I see losing love is like a window in your heart. Everybody sees you blown apart everybody sees the wind blow Graceland Graceland.*

I feel intoxicated by it all and the voice speaks out of tune, And I suppose this ain't Graceland, it says, as though concerned by it all. Well, I say in return, firmly and precisely, perhaps it is then perhaps it ain't whatever the case it's mine all the same, and they all look up from their laps and smile. My mam speaks, that is all well and good George but can we leave this place please its cold and unreal. My dad follows suit. Son you are closer to the truth than you think. That Ken was right Dad, all those years ago when he said all white people are racist. Henry is part of you as he is part of me but we refuse to accept it. You call it a grey area that has no place in the scheme of things and that's the truth of it all. The toing and froing in the old rocking chair is having an effect on my equilibrium.

Then why did you kill the round-faced black preacher man with the moustache? The voice asks. That wasn't me that was you. You found me in that dark place of a grave so who I've been since is simply down to you. There you go George, you are doing it again, they all sing in tune, blaming somebody else. You can shut your mouths, I scream, now I'm in the driving seat it is me taking control. So if a round-faced black man with a moustache, whoever he is, had to die, then so be it. All I ever wanted to do was sing like the King until now. Now the thing inside me is moving to fast, it feels out of control, or the other way round, who knows, it does, I hope.

Priscilla asks me in her own sweet way, Are you happy George? I can't tell, I reply with certainty. He has never been happy girl, Norm replies as if he was me and my dad nods his head and shakes Norm's hand as if he was his friend and my mam says, near to tears, and I don't know why that is. I do, the voice says, it's because he has never known who he truly is. It's since he's let that Fuller and that Priscilla get inside his head, my dad says. Norm jumps in, I agree, those two took him out of himself now he don't know the way back and he's near enough dead. Oh, but I do, Norman my friend, I do know the way back but the backs not there and I accept that fact. I am a bigot and hater of black skin; it's too late to change I know. He is just like his dad, the voice insists. In fact, his dad is me. My dad shouts, I resent that take it back. The voice says, I can't, it's your son that said it, not me.

Look, it doesn't matter no more this place is not what it seems. You are all here like it or not and I'm tired and too close to the end to do anything about what has been said and seen. So I think I'll go back and try to retrace my steps and start all over again. They all in chorus sing:

Pick yourself up brush yourself down and start all over again.

And they all laugh in perfect harmony with the voice breaking ranks to say: You can't, it's impossible to do, you killed the King remember. But how do I know? I reply. You don't, it says, but I do. Why do you want to go back? Priscilla asks, I'll take care of you here. We can make this place our home. But it's not what I thought it would be. And what was that? The voice asks. A place I have always wanted to be since I was twelve. But the graveyard is full of graves waiting to be filled don't let one be yours just yet, stay here with me. Norm chips in, for the time being at least. In fact it could be a respite for us all, Henry says smiling, I'm tired and I want to go home. Mae Ray is missing me. Yeah like a hole in the head, the voice says and Henry jumps in and shouts, yes and you know about that don't you killer cop cos Larry Payne said. Stop it you lot, I'm tired of you all and I sit here banging my head against a brick wall.

Memphis will thank you for it George, the voice whispers in my ear. It means now we can all get back to being us again. And what is that, pray? My mam interjects. Everything in its right place, everything as it should be, as God and nature intended, my dad proudly proclaims, balance restored you might say. And where do I stand in all this? My mam asks. You're here with me, my dad replies and he takes her hand in his and they both cry as my mam pulls her hand away and says, too late for all that now. I scream out, I'm Sorry please and I drift of to sleep, and leave with the bag still in my hand and Paul sings:

And sometimes when I'm falling, flying or tumbling in turmoil I say this is what she means we are bouncing into Graceland.

The rain has stopped. The air is fresh and I descend the cracked concrete steps and walk slowly to the back of the building, now derelict and beyond repair. A white picket lined fence is in the way so I jump it without effort and land amongst a clawing bramble thicket that seems determined to eat me for supper and would have if it hadn't released the green bag from my grip and ate that instead.

I run for my life, stumble and stop then move off again then stumble and stop some more. What is the point? I think. I am not getting anywhere. It is pitch-black and I cannot see a thing said the blind man to his deaf daughter. No point at all.

I lie down in a gap made by the bramble thicket and look up at the stars and wonder who else is doing the same. Somebody somewhere is doing the same, lying and looking up at the stars and lying to themselves in the process like all of us do in real time – spend our lives lying to others and more importantly to ourselves. Good old Doctor Foster who came from Gloucester just to see me says the exact same thing.

Elvis, he says, or, now you are nearly dead, should I call you George instead? Which one do you prefer? It is your call. It is too late in the day to argue. I say, my name is Elvis, and he says, Okay, Elvis it is. But I want you to consider that very thing that has put you in here which is the lying you have done to yourself.

No Doctor, I say, it is the drink that put me in here. I got drunk, too drunk for my own liking one night whilst I was out with my best friend Norm and I got so I couldn't remember the next morning what I did the night before. I didn't lie on purpose. Norm would vouch for that, if he had stayed on his feet but he didn't, did he doc, he fell like a ton of bricks. And now he's gone. And that makes me very sad. And there goes a shooting star. And Liza sings:

If they could see me now that little gang of mine dancing and prancing and drinking wine.

And there it is. I sit up and look in the direction of the light, a glimmer through a clump of trees. It twinkles like a guiding star. I wonder where you are, I shout and the voice inside my head says, you'd better get up and find out.

I smile, get to my feet and walk, stumble, you get the idea. The closer I get the bigger the light becomes, enormous like the moon and sun. I stumble over more greedy bramble thickets, my pit boots get stuck and I fall just as the ball of light splits and one becomes many and the many become torches and the torches have black faces attached.

I become frightened and freeze in my boots as the torches get closer and closer. They are looking for me; they are hunting me down; the voice has given them the lie it's a me it's a me it's a me my love standing in the cold cold rain. It's me; it's me they want to hang from the nearest tree.

But Doctor Foster, please tell me, do, who or what are my demons now? Well Elvis or is it George? It's George Doctor please. Well George the King is the biggest demon of all. But really, if you don't mind me saying, your demons are what you make them and you must find them and face them. But they are trying to hang me, like a piece of strange fruit. If I face them won't I die? Then so be it we will call it job done. I suppose so Doctor if I've got it to come. What does it matter how it happens? And I get the impression that it's starting to happen now.

I can hear angels singing and the lights have stopped moving and through the trees people are singing

If you miss me at the back of the bus and you can't find me nowhere come up to the front and you will find me there.

I move closer but they don't see me and I see Rosa Parks and I see my old man and Henry.

If you miss me at the picket line and you can't find nowhere come down to the court house, I'll be voting right there.

And they are crying and peering into an empty grave; a grave with my name on it. And I shout, No I'm here, but they don't respond. I push through and get stuck in a wall of black bodies and it begins to move and my feet are off the ground. I feel myself swaying

If you miss me in the cotton fields and you can't find me nowhere come on down to the jailhouse I'll be rooming in there.

Swaying with the tempo of shoeless feet and beating hearts.

Ain't going to let nobody turn me around turn me around turn me around.

And it stops and I fall and I keep falling into the open grave a long way down and I hear my name being spoken out loud for the whole world to hear. I open my eyes and Priscilla is smiling looking down at me. Am I dead? I say.

She is sitting next to the bed I am lying on. I ask her, Who are you smiling at? She doesn't answer. I try and get up but I am weak and fall back down again. A young black nurse comes up to the bed and takes my pulse. Amelia, I say and she smiles and says No, Jill. But you are not the Jill in my dreams and they both smile and the black lady says I can be if you want me to be it is entirely up to you, as she puts my arm back down and leaves.

I look at Priscilla and say to her, Are you who you say you are? I mean, your name, did they gave it you at birth? She nods her head and says, If I was to be a boy I probably would have been an Elvis like you. Both my parents were big fans and my dad; he was a singer like you.

My dad, I tell her, hated the man. Called him a waste of space, a boil on the backside of humanity is what he said. It was just you and your mum then? She says. Yes, thirty-first of December nineteen sixty-eight. I wasn't born then, she says, but my parents had him on tape. They've played it every Christmas since.

I liked it at Norm's house, I say, because his parents were always happy. They seemed to be always happy, she says, and it seemed your mum and dad weren't? But when you think it's the case you actually can't be sure. She was when I got up off the chair and sang his song cos she sang along with me and that was the first and last time that I sang in harmony with anybody.

But my dad he stayed unhappy for ever it seemed. He had his union. My mam had the King and I was wrapped up in cotton wool. The National Union of Mineworkers he was in and a shop steward to boot; a good one by all accounts. The revolution was always round the corner for him. You've got to be ready George, he'd always say. But I wasn't having any of it. I tried but the working class struggles he endlessly talked about weren't for me.

Then it all blew apart in eighty-four and I jumped ship, as they say. It didn't matter none to me. I was doing what I liked doing best. I'd put on the suits the King was in and become him.

Isn't he grand isn't he fine look at the cut the style the line.

Then I cry and nobody comes. They have all left me and time passes and I stop then and sit up to leave. My blue suede shoes are at the side of the bed. The ward is quiet again. I slide off the bed and onto the tall green chair next to it. I bend down and put on the shoes and walk out of the hospital with a distinct spring in my step.

It's a balmy night for January and I am feeling okay with myself. So I put one foot in front of the other and limp away.

One two buckle my shoe three four...

There is someone knocking at the door. George go see who that is please. Yes, can I help you? You certainly can George, you certainly can. Is your mother in George? Yes, she certainly is, why? Will you tell her that Mr Reaper, grim to you and me, is here to take her to the dance. But my dad is at work shouldn't we wait for him first? I'm sorry but these things happen, he says as he holds out his hands for me to take:

One two three, one two three one two three then you're out the door.

I cross the road on to Main, stop to get my bearings. Stop and get your bearings George and if you do get lost well don't panic just walk on and knock on the first door you come to. Yes young man, can I help you? I was out on my bike and now I'm lost, can you help me? I'll try, the tall lanky black man says. Tell me first where do you live? I don't know, is my reply and he says, Why don't you know, did you fall off your bike? That looks a nasty bump on your head.

Aren't you a bit, what should I say, strange to be out this late at night? Didn't your mammy tell you about the bogey men that live on the hill? I think she did, he says. Do I walk on or don't I. Go on son and don't stop I promise you will get there in the end. Your promises, I tell, him don't mean a thing. I have come across your sort before and he slams the door in my face.

Mister, you gotta a dollar to spare? And I tell the scraggy black man who is standing in front of me, hugging a brand new brush, No I have nothing but the blue suede shoes I am standing up in. I can sing, he shouts after me and I stop. Is that right? I ask. Yes sir and I can dance too, can you? And he and Mr Cohn is singing and dancing to the tune inside my head

Put on my blue suede shoes and I boarded the plane

I join in and we all sing

Touched down in the land of the Delta blues in the middle of the pouring rain

And people stop what they are doing to listen. He dances and I sing but what is coming out of my mouth doesn't sound nothing like the King. It doesn't sound like anything I have ever heard before. It doesn't sound like me that's for sure. I walk away with the man still singing inside my head.

Yeah I got a first class ticket but I'm as blue as a boy can be.

I tell myself familiarity breeds contempt. I'm feeling relaxed about it all. I enter the dance preparing myself for the worst or the best of things to come. The King is singing a sweet lament of times past and the light is on but the place is devoid of people making their way in and out but still looks inviting so I climb the steps and go in through the big glass doors that have Welcome written on them.

The light gets brighter as I get closer and I hear someone say, what is it you want from me? It's a man's voice and I can't make out if it's the King's or mine coming from under the illuminated spinning ball in the middle of the ballroom floor and the woman sings: I want you to be married to me to me I want you to be married to me George. The kids want a dad. What is one of them? I cry. I want George to penetrate me not a ghost who thinks he's real.

Listen Lorrie, listen. The illuminated light flickers and goes away leaving couples holding hands and kissing and the band swinging and the same people stop kissing and cuddling and start moving to the tune:

Sing sing sing sing everybody start to sing la dee da da ho ho ho now you're singing with a swing

My dad is throwing my mam over his young strong shoulders and through his legs and their feet don't touch the floor. They are smiling like I have never seen them smile before. I want to dance like them. George Proctor their son who is soon to be born and who has trouble putting one foot in front of the other now wants to dance before they break each other's heart.

I want to get onto my feet and shake a beat and dance away this crazy crazy, hang on… crazy what? Beat? No I have just said that. I can't say feet because that doesn't make sense. Not when you only have one good one: This crazy hazy day in a faraway summer way.

Stop it please. See now I have lost the impetus and the music goes on without me. I am just watching the last bus home leave and I am not on it. See, the trouble with you George. His words ring in my ears. Yes Dad I shout. You've got no get up and go inside. Then his words disappear like the lost chord did many years ago. So I get up and go and I leave. I go out the door and back on to the road going north and the voice screams Elvis! Elvis! Elvis!

I don't turn round I let the voice come to me. I say, lose some weight, in an arrogant sort of way, even though it scares me, even though it's me. It laughs and between its deep breaths it says, you are so right Elvis, everybody says the same.

I walk on and the voice stays and says, Sorry about the hospital bit and I stop and ask it, how did you know? And it says, I know Elvis because it was me that tripped you up and it was me that picked you up and it was me that got you to the hospital and got you onto a bed.

Its breathing is easing and I straighten up. For a fat man with a gammy leg I seem taller than before. I'm sorry and thanks and I walk on. It shouts after me, you don't have to thank me Elvis. I stop walking and say to myself, what else could I do? I had a dream.

But George how do you know they are dreams? I stop and turn and stare through a window at a reflection that looks like me but I'm not sure. There is a blank look behind his black, black eyes that I haven't noticed before. Hey George, tell me the difference between being awake and being asleep. Two worlds that collide and make one, is that it? You tell me. You have lived in both all your life which one of them is you in now.

But sometimes one supersedes the other without you knowing. Do you know what I mean? Have you, George Proctor, been living your dream or just living a lie? Is Memphis your dream or just a fantasy? You tried to be a king but instead you finished up killing one. Well it happens and you've got to ask yourself why because it is your dream, your property.

Now you are creeping me out whatever your name is, and I walk on hoping it will leave me alone but it don't. Leave me alone, I scream. I can't, it screams back, unless you decide otherwise, what is yours is mine.

I stop and walk back to the mirrored wall and look through. There is a kind of serenity in his eyes now. What you mean by that? I ask and he smiles. What I said George. It's your decision, you decide, do I stay or do I go? Am I dreaming now? Give me a sign please. Because how on God's earth would I know about the King if you weren't there to tell me. The eyes smile back and ask, you tell me, you tell me the truth whatever that is and then, hopefully, there will be peace.

There will be peace in the valley for me

And you because we are both tired and we are both weary and we both want to go home.

Lorrie left me and took the kids and went with him. It was his fault. So I hit him. He hit the floor like a sack of spuds and didn't move. I stood over him like a victor does. I nudged his leg with mine but he didn't stir. So I bent down. My face was a fraction away from his and I whispered in his ear, Ever seen somebody crying for mercy Norm? Bang pow they hit the floor like a bag of spuds your knuckles are ripped but it doesn't matter cos you are feeling good inside bang bang bang. Your whole body is moving fuelled with hate; there is no escape, cos you are hooked. Violence is everywhere, the night air is oozing blood, screaming bodies heaving, heads cracking, open legs flying in all directions then one last moan before the big sleep then you die. What's your game pal? Which side are you on boy? My old man said. Which side are you on and I screamed an unconditional scream, you what you what you what you what you what, and I walk away feeling good with myself and not caring a toss about the consequences of it all. Was it because Norm was black I ask myself or because he stole my wife and kids.

Memphis has swallowed me up before the parasite has eaten away my insides. So it doesn't matter no more. I have been to the mountain top and seen the Promised Land. I just got to keep on walking till the battle's done. Then I can go home and rest but not yet because if Memphis is my dream and the fat man is right then I am in control of my own destiny. The future is mine to mess up as I wish.

I wish for Priscilla. I want Priscilla. I want to lay next to her, feel her young soft body next to mine. Lay your head on my pillow, your warm and tender body next to mine for the last time possibly.

But where shall I find my Priscilla? Where will Priscilla be? More importantly where will the baby's thimble be? Is it Bill or is it Ben? Tomorrow will take care of itself. My mam was always saying it. George stop your worrying son because tomorrow never comes.

I walk down Main to Beale. The nearer I get the more Elvi's I see. Beale Street is Memphis Tennessee. There wouldn't be a Memphis if it wasn't for Beale. That's what Henry says anyways. The black man built Memphis, lived, sang and made love on Beale. Beale is the pulsating heart and spirit of Memphis. That is what he says. Without it the rest would just wither away and die.

Like it nearly did in the seventies when some of the city folk wanted to knock it down and build office blocks and apartments. We told them city folks you can't dance and sing and laugh about office blocks and apartments, no sir, so they got wise to where the money really is and here it is on Beale. It's my place to rest awhile and think of Mae Ray.

I walk down Beale and there she is sitting high on a bar stool sipping an ice cool beer; corny or what? I stand looking at her listening to the singer sing his song: lay your head on my pillow put you warm and tender body next to mine for the last time and I get bumped I turn around to face Priscilla smiling at me.

She takes my hand and pulls me along the streets of Beale and on to Fourth Avenue. Look Elvis, she says, the crossroads of life. I tell her to call me George: a pub, church, school and pawn shop just like home and a car pulls up beside us and its doors open and Priscilla gently eases me onto the back seat. Henry is driving. You remember the church hall where you sang your first and only song.

I can smell her next to me and she smells of Magnolia, her long red hair hangs loose close to my head and I have an urge to bury my face into it, to die here with her hair choking the life out of me, gently choking the life out of me. She is still holding my hand and I squeeze it and her squeezes mine back.

Henry turns the taxi right onto Union Avenue. The people have gone and the sun shines bright on our happy happy home. Henry shouts *I Am A Man* and I say Amen to all that. Priscilla squeezes my hand some more and says so are you.

I feel relaxed and ahead of us I can see an illuminating fluorescent light high in the sky shining like a star and as we get closer Priscilla and Henry sing:

And I join in and we are all in perfect harmony with Henry on the top note and Priscilla underneath and the sun it shines some more on our happy sunny home and the car stops and the doors open and Priscilla eases me off the back seat with Henry following and Priscilla still holding and squeezing my hand says, I understand.

We walk through the green door and into the room I am writing this in. A shining bare light hangs from the ceiling like the one above me is doing now. A double bass and two guitars, one electric the other acoustic, lean against the bright white wall under a small window that has a blue curtain drawn across it. Like the one you can see if you turn around.

Henry, without saying a word, picks up the double bass and begins: dum dum dum dum dum dum dum dumming it. Priscilla, pretty as a picture Priscilla, does likewise with the electric guitar: dum dum dum dum dum dum dum dum and me, well, I pick up the acoustic and join in.

Well that's all right Mama that's all right with you that's all right Mama any way will do.

And it is in this bright white front room where everything is okay de de de de de de de de de

I want your loving.

I am surrounded by ghosts knocking out tunes on the old battered brown piano that sits in the corner of the room making a mark on the white wall as it does so. The King dressed immaculately in his new long brown coat is sitting on the stool and smiling singing in tune with Carl and Jerry Lee with Jerry desperately trying to pinch the young man's crown. I am in heaven and I don't want it to end.

But it does and leaves a hollow inside that you know will not be filled ever again. I have to hang on to my fantasies because it is all I've got. They are what make the thought of dying real and I am not afraid anymore because I am walking in Memphis with my two feet off the ground. So the song goes.

But it is only a song. I know that now. Memphis though has given me more than one King with each doing their best to claim it their own. I have stepped out of a giant shadow and back into my own skin what is left of it that is. The fat man has given me the key to the green door and the secrets it was hiding, mine. I am truly sorry about Norm. He was truly my friend. Like they say in the song:

You always hurt the one you love. The one you never hurt before.

And sleep overtakes me again. I wake overlooking Lauderdale. The acned fair-haired young boy is still there sitting alone strumming a tune on an old battered acoustic guitar. His fate awaits him. I stand and stare at a life that is full of care and Norman stands with me and reads his favourite poem. I can see the cold finger pointing at me through the big pane of glass darkly.

Through the mist a dustbin lorry sits quietly waiting for the rain to stop. Henry, wearing his new green tweed suit is lining up dustbins at the side of the road. They are there ready for his two mates to collect but they don't turn up. A loud penetrating *Tap! Tap! Tap!* wakes me into a world from a long long way back.

I am dressed in blue jeans, shirt and dad's full length coat that smells of rotting fish down to my shins. I lift the window away from the sash and climb onto the scullery roof and down its pipe onto the snow hard ground and up the entry with Norm behind.

Have you got it? He hisses through chattering teeth.

In the pitch black night under the street lamp I open wide my dad's heavy coat and show him the spade.

We turn off Sydenham Street into Croydon Road and skip through the twitchel onto Hartley Road and it is freezing brass monkeys in the crumbling old Radford churchyard.

A heavy sweet smell of tobacco from the factory close by swims over the graves and hits us hard.

It smells like my old man, Norman says.

She's over there, I splutter.

Where?

There near the stair at the back of the church.

I drag Norm, stumble and fall, to the nearly visible Widow Grace's freshly dug grave (1880-1962) and take out the spade from under the coat.

Are you sure?

As apples aren't oranges and oranges aren't fruit, I reply through unfeeling teeth.

I slam down the sharp end of the spade onto the rock hard soil of the grave and a loud thud echoes near waking the dead and my hand shakes uncontrollably and my head splits in two.

I mean, she ain't been gone more than a week.

And she'll be gone next week and the week after that, I say cursing his voice.

The clock strikes ten.

Despite the death defying freeze my head is sweating and the soil's not moved. The old Radford church is singing the blues and a light from a torch has replaced the moon.

Heavy giant footsteps pound the Church Lane field.

It's him, it's him, it's him again.

It might not be I whisper unreassuringly whilst lying poleaxed across widow Grace's grave.

The flashlight beam floats above my head and sits winking long before it moves away and a gate squeaks.

A deep voice thunders. Say goodnight boys. Wee Willy is coming to get you.

We scarper fast back down Hartley Road leaving the spade and don't stop running till we hear the Plough Inn spilling its guts all over the place.

My dad's bulky frame falls from the Plough into St Peter's Street.

I grab Norm's oversized mac and drag him over the rickety old bridge that covers the cold unfriendly Leen. We crouch with the trolls underneath and my old man bellows out as only he can with his Frankie Vaughan voice for Widow Grace to hear:

All I want to do is join the happy crowd…

Stop! Stop! Stop! Please!

It's eleven o'clock.

Listen George—

What—

It's the ticking of the clock. You are getting close—

Yes, I silently scream.

My old man has stopped. A lifetime passes before I can poke my head above the bridge and survey the dark cold night scene.

I don't feel well. I want to be sick.

Norm gets up with the rising of the sun and takes a look.

See what you mean pal. I see what you mean. One house is standing alone in the middle of the road and it's yours, he says, close to my ear.

I know one derelict house with green doors one two three four.

Norm screams inside my head. What now George? What now?

The clock strikes twelve.

I pee myself and say through foggy eyes, I know Norm let's count to eight, play hide and seek and start again.

Why eight, he asks scared stiff of ghosts he might see.

I don't know—

You knew about the secret thing that was buried with widow Grace.

I know, my old man said in his sleep one day, after the pit shut down for good, pieces of eight pieces of eight. He called her a witch when he couldn't get his own way.

But she was my widow Grace not his.

Eight! Waste! Time and place.

It is all waste now but for the mean derelict house with its green burnt stained doors.

Which way now George, which way?

I turn half circle and see beyond the bridge an old round brick building in a lake.

The clock strikes eight.

It's a near folly-shaped waste, battered by age, I say. Radford pit, once upon a time, before yours and mine stood there too, after like—

See, you do know everything. So, George, north south east or west—

It don't matter none to me it's all the bleeding same.

The clock strikes eight.

The four doors open slowly, each one beckoning in their own cruel way. I turn to run as the hot sun sits itself above the holy roof and the lonely house below sings *The Old Rugged Cross*, my mam's favourite tune. The one the King sang

Norm grabs my arm. There is no escape now, he whispers through his now toothless grin.

And the church bells strike eight again.

I can't move and he strokes my hair with his thick black hand.

The grown-ups have sussed us. It's time to give in.

My old, now finally dead, crumbling body feels secure. It is firmly fixed to the spot and refuses to budge as if stuck in mud. It's got lost, sunk nowhere now to be found amongst the sheets and pillows wet with decrepit sweat.

I am drowning in tears from days past spent. I forget where I am: Norm's gone. It was my fault I know that now. I'm to blame and there is no way out.

That smell of Magnolia haunts my nose and a sweet voice and gentle hand mops my now dead brow. Wake up George, the voice says softly in my shrivelled ear. It is past eight o'clock and breakfast is served: sunny side up just how you like it.

POSTSCRIPT

I turned over the last page and sat back, feeling exhausted. I just wanted to get home. I leant back on the chair and suddenly realised how dark it had become. I looked at my watch, but it had stopped. I could hear the rain. I got up from the chair intending to leave. Instead I walked back to the window and looked out. Our backyard had been the same as this one. I could see myself as a young boy kicking a ball up against the side of the house and hearing my dad yelling from the bedroom window. He would have been on nights and trying to get some sleep. He was a miner.

I walked back to the table and gathered together the manuscript. Suddenly, the bare light above my head went on. I could hear faint footsteps behind the door opposite me. The door opened on to some stairs that led up to the bedrooms. I knew this because I had grown up in a house like this one. I left when I got married some thirty years ago. We are divorced now. We have been for a long time. I don't see the kids anymore

The door opened and a young woman entered. Her

hair was long and black, hanging down on each side of her face. She wore a purple flowered dress that hung below her knees. I watched her walk to the chair opposite me, pull it away from the table and sit down. She crossed her legs and pulled her dress up over her knees. She smiled a beautiful smile. I couldn't stop myself from looking at the photograph on the mantelpiece of the young woman standing next to the man in a mohair suit.

"You have read it then?" She asked. "I told George you would."

I looked at her hard and said, "Priscilla."

She smiled.

"I thought Priscilla was a figment of his imagination," I said, still staring hard into her eyes.

"We are all a figment of somebody's imagination, don't you think, David? I was George's carer and his lover and his mother. In the world that surrounds you I was his carer. In George's world in front of you I was his lover and his mother."

"And how long have you been upstairs?" I asked

her, not believing that she could have been up there all the time I was reading.

"Forever", she said smiling

"Forever? What a strange answer."

"The truth all the same."

"Whose truth, though, I wonder? Tell me, Priscilla, the other people in the story besides you and George?

Now she was looking hard at me, as though she was searching for something deep inside. She was still smiling that most beautiful smile. A few seconds passed in silence.

"George went to Memphis to fulfil his dream. He did sing his song and while he was there he did meet Henry. He came back home with the cancer determined to have its own way and with Henry's and his dead friends' words, eating into his brain: George, we said, in 1968 you took a wrong turn and you've been trying to get back ever since, but you didn't know how and you didn't know why and you didn't know which road to take. George died knowing Henry was right and that is all that matters. What you have just read is George's journey back home and that is all he wanted."

Looking at her I could see why George was smitten with her.

"His dead friends…"

She shrugged her shoulders.

"You haven't read the manuscript then?

"No, of course I haven't. You are the only one to have had that privilege. I kept his fingers moving and his heart beating"

I was too tired to get into a long conversation with her. I just wanted to leave. I stood up.

"Okay, Priscilla, tell me why me?" I fastened up my big coat, wrapping it around me as tight as I could.

"George said that you would understand. He found your name and telephone number amongst Norman's possessions and kept it. Norm had told him that you were a nice fellow – a good man, a genuine man."

"What?" I said it louder than I intended to, she had taken me by surprise. "Those are big statements from somebody I hardly knew."

"Well, George believed him, took him at his word because Norm was George's only friend, but he betrayed him.

I nodded. "Yes it happens", I said.

"Yes and it was George that killed him".

I shook my head in disbelief. I had no idea what to say. I stood looking at the manuscript.

"I'm a busy man."

"We are burying him the day after tomorrow."

"We? I thought he had nobody else?"

"He has me and he has Henry and his friends. Will you come? He would like to see you there"

"I don't know," was my immediate reply.

She got up and walked back towards the stairs. I had the urge to follow her.

"Yes you do," she said matter of factly.

She took the first step and I whispered, "I'm sorry."

She turned slightly and looked over her shoulder at me and smiled. I could see she was with child.

"you're pregnant"

"Yes we will call it David"

The door closed behind her and the light went out. I could hear her faint footsteps climbing the stairs. In my mind, I heard my mother shouting, "Don't forget to turn the light off before you come up." And then all I could hear was the rain falling. I dropped back onto the chair and waited for the darkness.

There is nothing in the dark that isn't there when the lights are on.....Rod Serling

DEDICATED TO

The Sanitation workers of 1968 for making a stand

George Proctor, comrade and friend

Norman Hall my lifelong friend who died before his time

And Isla, my beautiful young granddaughter, who takes me into her own imaginative world and teaches me how to play.

I WANT TO THANK

June West and Pallas Pidgeon, of The Memphis Heritage for their warm welcome and for giving up their time to chat

Michael Honey for writing and publishing 'Going Down Jericho Road'

Joan Turner Beifuss for writing and publishing 'At the River I Stand' Both are superb books about the sanitation workers strike

The California Newsreel company for sending me their film also named 'At the River I stand'

My family for keeping me going

Gavin Morgan for a superb cover design

Gillian Holmes my editor for putting me right.

Lightning Source UK Ltd.
Milton Keynes UK
UKOW02f0603071116
286994UK00001B/4/P